BLUE

a steamy erotic romance

Bronwen Pryce

Blue Mountain Books
an imprint of DBP Press

2015

BLUE

a steamy erotic romance

Bronwen Pryce

Blue Mountain Books
an imprint of DBP Press

2015

BLUE

Printed in the United States of America.
First Printing (eBook), 2014. Second Printing, 2015.

ISBN 978-0692430064

Blue Mountain Books c/o DBP Press
Post Office Box 399 | Tarpon Springs, FL 34688

Always for She, to whom I belong.

AUTHOR'S FOREWORD

As a writer of sensual, sexy, and pornographic fiction for both sexes (and multiple sexual proclivities), I've added to my list of published titles very slowly and quite sporadically. After fifteen years, I discovered how best to put these separate short pieces together. As opposed to an anthology, I put them into a cohesive single story set in the foothills of northern Georgia, the Appalachian Mountains, and my fantasy version of the Blue Ridge Parkway—a trilogy I call my **Deep BLUE Three**.

BLUE is the first of the three distinct yet interconnected parts. On the surface, it is a hot, erotic romance about two people trying to revisit the past and repair a broken relationship. Beneath the surface, however, BLUE initiates a pornographic exploration of how men and women are affected by the taboo, desire and lust, human sexuality, sin and regret, pain and pleasure, and the insanity of love's exhaustive litany of crippling labors.

I've always viewed sexual activity with inconstant eyes. I'm a great admirer of the experience, as a whole, but I've never embraced the finer (or baser) aspects of the driving impulse we all share. I've been accused of committing "Serial Monogamy" more often than not, but still I've enjoyed my fair share of sexual entertainments, despite the lack of variety. In practice, marrying carnal fantasy to sexual reality fills me with dread and suspicion, which is why I set my brain on fire before I creatively explore that arena.

That my mind is so willing to delve the deepest caverns of my dark imaginings doesn't surprise me. That it uncovers so many strange thoughts and ideas does. Lipstick lesbian this girl may be, I proudly hail from a traditional family wrought from the forges of middle America—I'm not one of the strange fruits that fell off some Dionysian cult family tree back in 1970s San Francisco.

Giving my thoughts free reign allows me to contemplate all the facets of sexuality without feeling guilty about giving in to a secret, unexplored desire. Not every sexual fantasy should be experienced first-hand, but that shouldn't preclude frank discussions, conversations, and storytelling. Remember, the mind usually turns on before the body does. Toward that end, I prefer my naughty stories with a plot and believable characters. Without a proper framework for the myriad acts of hot steamy sex, however arousing those acts may be, what else is there to keep the reader engaged.

Without a sense of time and place, without danger or consequences, without drama or humor, without that taut feeling of slow building tension and cruel anticipation, *why would anyone bother with words when there are millions of free X-rated videos online?* At the risk of sounding like Jack Horner, the avuncular porn director in *Boogie Nights*, I want my naughty story to suck you in and hold your interest, make you keep turning pages, carry you beyond orgasm until you get to the glorious climax of the story, and then ease your way to the very last sentence. It is my sincerest desire that BLUE will do exactly that for you and pique your interest enough to continue the journey with me.

— *Bronwen Pryce, October 2014*

EPIGRAPH

In secret we meet
In silence I grieve,
That thy heart could forget,
Thy spirit deceive.
If I should meet thee
After long years,
How should I greet thee?
With silence and tears.

— Lord Byron

It is a matter of an education. I will put into their pretty little heads every principle of the most unbridled of libertines. I will set them ablaze with fire, feeding them upon our philosophy, inspire them with our desires. As I wish to join practice to theory, as I like the demonstrations dedicated to the roses of Sodom, I'll have two pleasures at once: that of enjoying these lecheries myself, and that of giving the lessons inspiring such fancies to those I lure into my net.

— Marquis de Sade

Departure

The wonder of it all, this tasting you
Gliding, sliding slipping in my tongue feeds
My need to knead this bliss by kissing through
A free-fall moment to take that, which bleeds.

—Simone Simon, from *Precipice*

A FROSTY, SOPPY ASHEVILLE MORNING. We leave the hotel at nine, sans breakfast and hungover as hell. She's wearing a snow bunny outfit, replete with faux fur boots.

I'm wearing the prize I won in last night's karaoke contest. A leather bomber jacket, replete with sexy decals, for singing 60s do-wop in some hotel bar. Meghan's still impressed. She calls me dashing and handsome in brown leather. And despite my pounding head, I feel dashing and handsome, and quilted cozy warm.

We leave the parking lot. She gazes at me with her blue-gray Civil War colored eyes, big and liquid eyes. Eyes I think I want to see every day of my life. Her slightly hungover happy face is lost in the memory of last night.

I know I'm lost in the memory of it.

A cool king-sized bed. Candles and incense, a crackling fire. The hurricane lamp by the window glowing soft above sounds of jazz wafting up like smoke from the stereo. A bottle of wine, her glowing skin. And my hands running fingers across her waist, her thighs, the backs of her knees, the spot on her right ankle that makes her giggle when I tickle it. The place behind her neck, right under the hair at the nape of it that sprouts goose flesh at the slightest touch. It makes her coo and moan, and it makes me warm to think of her moaning. And it's hard not to think of her moaning.

I'm warm all over now, warm like lust and love. Her hand finds mine as we drive and remember. I look at her, and she's grinning at me madly, musically, magically.

As much as I need to see her face—those eyes, those lips, that mouth—I'm driving and need to keep us alive until we stop again. Until we fuck again. Taste each other again. Get lost until we both forget, once again, why we're driving the Blue Ridge Parkway. That we're trying to rekindle love as we traverse this mountain pass.

The road is a winding one. The drive is long and slow. And we say nothing as we head southwest into the rolling, icy fog covering the mountain.

What do we say to each other?

Not much.

After days of rolling around in our ocean of endless fucking, words are useless and silly. Once again, our first moments in today's drive quell the violent ebb and flow of our continually renewed lusts. We fill comfortable silences with small talk and gossip.

We avoid the heavy stuff for now.

There's a price for these omissions, as we are still floundering and flailing for the intimacy we crave, the bond we never had. It's more difficult than I thought it would be. I want to tell her this, but I don't know how to make the words sound like I'm not trying to break her down, which she fears and hates.

And so, we head blindly into the fog of love and war.

Memory dwells here—the past, the haze of pain all but forgotten, if not forgiven. In the haze, we are new again, fragile and all-too-eager to be better than we once were, but still fearful of what we'll become. So, we don't talk about what we so need to talk about. We hold hands like teenagers, fondle and tease each other, watch the fog play between the cars and trucks accompanying us on the Parkway. With the radio off, all we can hear is the crackling tires, a humming engine, and our sighs of fearful fire.

*

We stop for breakfast at a little old gas station restaurant. We eat quickly and then take a stroll to the natural overlook at the end of a narrow, wooded trail. We're alone. With the fog thinning and the sun peeking, the view is beautiful. We hold each other as we take it all in. I think to myself that this is a good thing, this reunion after our two-year breakup. I feel her thinking the same thing as she clings to me. Our heat rises in smoky vapor as we press closer. She kisses my neck and moves a hand around to my backside.

She kisses my neck again.

"Joss Parker, I love how you smell," Meghan tells me, and I believe her. Taking my hand, she unzips the front of her pants and slips it inside. "Only you can make me this wet," she says, lifting up slightly to open up for my finger to slide in as she comes down slowly on it. "Well, isn't that nice. If people were to come up here and see us like this—like that nice old man behind you—they'd never know your finger was all up in me."

"There's nobody behind me."

"Good morning, you two young people," a voice says behind me. Sauntering toward the far corner of the platform, oblivious to our secret situation, an older man with a walking stick passes us by.

Meghan giggles, tells me to keep quiet as she rearranges herself to a more respectable woman, and turns around to greet our latest arrival. Of course, she's rubbing her well-rounded rump back and forth on my poor hard cock, the naughty minx. And then she leaves me to go talk to the nice gentleman in the hound's-tooth cap.

With a grin, I lift my cool, drying finger and breathe in her smell. I think of last night, and the night before that, and the morning before that. Yes, dear God, that morning, when we fucked in a pool of sunlight pouring in from the bedroom window the morning we left Atlanta for Asheville. When she looked at me with those amazing eyes bright with sun and love, I screamed and emptied myself on her stomach and thighs, and the folds of her pussy. How she played in it with her fingers, rolling her glistening digits on the tip of her tongue, smiling at me as I fell.

Oh, how I did fall.

And as I look at her with the old man now, I know I'm still falling. I'm falling again, and I know it's dangerous and I don't care. I don't care, and I'm glad I don't know the way of all reunions with Meghan. Hope is a fucking hindsight bitch, isn't it?

We make our way back to the car.

Meghan gives me that "knowing" look. You know the look. And I can't stop thinking of how nice it would be for a once-more-into-the-king-sized-bed-dear-friends-once-more kind of fuck. A grinding, dirty, quick one with blue talk and loud screams. The cave sex of eager bodies, pulsing organs, filthy mouths.

She is looking at me and telling me this with her blue eyes until the words seep from her lips in sweet wisps. Lips pure and innocent until you've seen them kissing their way from chest to stomach and then set loose upon your cock.

Move your hair, I can't see.

You like to watch, don't you?

Yes, God, you know I do.

"You look so goddamn good in your jacket," she says to me. "Just know how much I want you as we drive through the mountains."

By three o'clock, we're pulling into the parking lot of the mountain lodge we found on Trip Advisor. The Parkway will take us to our final overnight stay in Cherokee tomorrow night.

Today, however, in the very rustic hunting lodge looming to our immediate right, there's a motorcycle convention.

Older people on motorcycles and in sidecars. Headgear with attached over-the-ear microphone headsets. Shiny matching travels suits and helmets. The motorcyclists are older, next-door neighbor-types. Baby boomers mostly, the kind of folks who run Mom-n-Pop shops during the week and disappear into roving packs of geriatric bikers over the weekend.

"Looks like we're going to make new friends," Meghan sings. "Let's check in."

"But I'm about to go insane from a swollen blue scrotum."

My snow bunny giggles. "And you have to wait for my healing touch," she says. "I mean, look where we are—we have plenty of time for us. I'd like to see what these strangers are all about. Think of the stories they could tell us." With a slight twist, she shimmies her rump like Marilyn Monroe. "I love stories, don't you?"

"You're teasing me, and I don't like you very much!"

Meghan looks at me sideways. "Why, Joss Parker, I'm sure I don't know what you're talking about." She walks off toward the lobby in a sexy pout to get our room key.

*

The Meeting

Your wet glass of beauty, your fractured pearl—
O, to milk a growl from your other lips.

—Simone Simon, from *Precipice*

MY BALLS ARE NEARLY INSIDE MY BODY. A desperate moan, a sudden arc of my back, and I'm rigid, and then flat on the bed again, my head tossing from side to side.

A second louder moan announces a sudden shot of warm white liquid from the head of my penis, which hits the headboard behind me with a tiny little smack. Amidst several ensuing encore groans and moans, I start laughing.

Meghan milks another shot and giggles when the line falls across the length of my torso, from my belly button to my suprasternal notch, a long pearly string glistening like a swath of Elmer's glue on my chest. "My goodness," she says, squeezing out the last drips of cum until my throbbing finally subsides. "You hit the goddamn headboard."

I'm still laughing. "I hit the goddamn headboard."

Meghan gets up from the bed. "I'll get a washcloth—you must've needed that one."

I don't deny it, but I'm too dumb and dizzy to make the words.

An hour later, we're dressed for dinner, looking like a royal fucking flush as we walk arm in arm into the fancy restaurant in the lobby downstairs. After a magnificent steak and lobster dinner, we saunter to the rustic hunting lodge-themed lounge and sit at the piano bar for cocktails. A table opens up for us near the stuffed grizzly bear mounted on a tall wooden block with several posed taxidermified beavers, possums, and skunks.

We sit down at our little candlelit table for two.

And that's when we see Gary and Carol Rider. We haven't been introduced yet, but we will be soon enough. And I'd rather dispense with unnecessary mystery and say the names of the two unbelievably magnetic people, Carol and Gary.

They are sitting at a large table on the platform behind us. Carol's laughter is brash and spirited in a Martha-from-Who's-Afraid-of-Virginia-Woolf kind of way. I mean, we hear it and immediately turn toward the buxom, Southern, and oh so matronly woman behind the alarming sound.

Carol Rider is a gum chewing Chatty Cathy with beehive hair and Miss Piggy-blue eye shadow. Her polka dot cocktail dress hugs her mighty-mighty brick house of a body like the new skin of a sexy snake. And she's decked in bangles and fat round beads, and she shines like a slice of Indian summer sun. Carol is a bona fide, card-carrying sexpot, oozing sultry, sensual heat, and she's genuinely oblivious to it—that's power.

"She's goddamn sexy," Meghan whispers to me. "Right?"

I can only nod. Of course, she's right, but I'm too transfixed to speak. There's a small crowd around these two people and I want to know why.

Ah, Carol's telling a story. "And so, after hauling the chocolate brown calf from the pool and out the lanai, the short cowboy in charge shifts his lasso to shake Gary's hand and give him his card. He apologizes for waking us up and offers to pay for repairs."

Carol is on fire. "We had the screens repaired and the pool cleaned—that fucking cow made a huge expensive mess—so, we called the number that bastard dwarf gave us, and I swear the son of a bitch had his phone disconnected to avoid paying for the damages!"

The crowd roars with laughter and applause. When the noise dies down, the people gathered there finally leave the couple to their drinks and search for other stories to hear. And no wonder—the place is packed to the rafters. Who would've thought a tiny place tucked in a nook off the Blue Ridge Parkway would be so popular?

I didn't give it a thought.

I'm still transfixed to the beautiful older couple glowing like a pair of shamans over there.

"I think Gary is sexier than Carol," Meghan whispers.

She may be right about that, but I'm still lost in staring at them.

For several moments, Carol and Gary aren't aware of the two younger people gawking in silent awe. But then, without any warning, Gary catches my eye, raises his whiskey glass, and winks.

And then I understand what Meghan means.

For all of Carol's sublime sound and delightfully animated fury, Gary is the one who pulls you into orbit around the two of them. He's the one who charms you, the one who galvanizes all your curiosity, the one who hypnotizes you. He's Paul Newman and Cary Grant and Robert Redford all mixed together, baked to a tanned bubbly, and slathered with George Clooney frosting.

I want to introduce myself, but Meghan beats me to the punch.

Our table is on a platform half a foot beneath theirs, and we have to stand at the railing separating us to chat. Meghan is great at this kind of thing, and soon the two women are laughing and carrying on like sisters. Gary and I are making small talk, and I have a feeling that he is sizing me up, studying me. He has this incredible intensity, a directness that disarms you as it draws you in, a candor of speaking, a focus that makes you feel you are the most important person in the room—Gary has dangerous charisma. I have no idea who this man and woman are. I only have a feeling about them.

I have no fucking idea what I'm feeling or why, but I feel something in my gut. Something deep and powerful, and beyond intuition is telling me my life and everything in it is about to change.

Oddly enough, our conversation begins in polite, almost Victorian tones, but the more we imbibe and smoke, the easier it is to move past the small talk. About an hour into our genial back and forth, we join forces at a table in the corner close to the fireplace and away from the fucking bear. The conversation takes on a life of its own. We open up to each other. By the evening's end, you would have thought the four of us were lifelong best friends. They told us, slurred and silly and drunkenly delirious how they were taking the Blue Ridge Parkway back to their home in Cherokee.

Coincidence? That's what I'm thinking.

Later, of course, I'll rethink that and everything else about Gary and Carol. And even Meghan. But like I said, I don't know things are about to change.

"So, how did you two meet?" I ask.

Gary looks at Carol. The top of her dress is coming undone around her left breast. He lovingly adjusts it, tapping the pearl necklace draped below her chin, as he says, "We met at a sex club in Cleveland, Ohio, in 1977."

Meghan leans forward, spills her drink. "That can't be true."

I look at my unsteady girl and settle her upright in her chair. I narrow my eyes at Gary, then Carol, chiming in with her singsong addendum: "We really did. Don't blame us—it was the 70s, we were young—"

"The pot and blow," Gary says with a laugh, "and you can blame me for all of that."

Carol kisses Gary's neck. "Oh, that mustache of yours."

Gary chuckles. "She was there with another guest too," he says, craning his head around to add, "Elton John glasses and a feather boa, right?"

"Oh, he was a pretty mister Miss Kitty," Carol says. "I wore my best Janis Joplin denim jeans, wrapped me a long scarf 'round my bosom for a top. Well, the invite called for celebrity attire. Who'd a thought Cleveland would be a hotspot for orgies?"

"Wanna hear the story?" Gary asks. "Good. I'd just turned eighteen. I was young and out of work and needed some quick cash. Disco clubs in those days were the rage, but this one place did something different. The owner offered me a lot of money to work for him that one night. And what a night it was."

Carol giggles. "Kiddies, Studio 54 came to Middle America," she says, her bracelets and earrings clinking as she scoots her chair closer. She shifts toward Gary and continues the story with conspirator's smile. "I had no idea what to expect—after all, I was barely eighteen and in love with a bisexual dancer named Thomas. He was the one in the boa, by the way. Anyway, we just moved to Cleveland from Pensacola when he gets an invitation to this secret disco club downtown. Meghan, honey, your Jossie here looks just like my Thomas—young, blond, cleft in his chinny-chin-chin, hazel eyes, strong arms, chiseled."

Meghan smiles, rubs the inside of my thigh. "He sounds

yummy," she says, kissing my ear. "My baby's built like a Greek fucking god too."

"He most certainly is," Carol says. "Anyway, Thomas and I go to this old factory. We're high as kites and horned up, and we stand in this line for an hour before it starts moving. We're in the front middle of the line now, and it keeps growing as more people in costumes come. Lots of young men in drag, lots of young men in next to nothing too. Girls in Scarlet O'Hara gowns, Annie Oakley western wear, Judy Garland Dorothy dresses and pigtails—God only knows what they had in those picnic baskets. Anyway, the anticipation was killin' us—two men got out of line and went at each other right there on the asphalt."

"They were done waiting," Gary says with a chuckle. "Fools."

Carol nods, snaps her fingers for another Long Island Iced Tea. "Indeed, we all were feelin' frisky, but waitin' for the door to open was better than sex. The line moves, and the man at the door was lettin' folks in or tellin' them to leave."

"Why's that?" I ask.

"There was a password," Gary replies, a grin on his face. "And take a wild guess as to who was standing at the door. Yep, I was the gatekeeper. Wore nothing but a trench coat too, but I was tall and hairy enough to look older than I was."

Carol hums in her husband's ear. "You were such a fox."

Gary blushes, rolls his eyes, continues, "The passwords were 'rooster', 'cogburn', 'john wayne', 'eye patch', and 'true grit'. I sent lots of people away that night."

"Not me," Carol says with a groan, straightening when the server brings her drink. "Ah, this is the stuff, kiddies. So, Thomas and I go inside. Disco is pumping through all the different rooms, each one has a bar and dance floor. Mirrors for walls. Beanbags and old leather sofas. Incense, pot, candles, fake fog—smoke is everywhere. The rooms up front are slowly filling because everyone else is in the back room. People are lounging over each other and on the furniture. Even more are grinding on the dance floor. Thomas kissed me on the cheek and left me at the bar. I stood there watching this scene unfold. Completely turned on and utterly terrified to do anything about it. I only just had my cherry popped a few months earlier, so I was happy to observe. There was this one young woman, Dorothy Gale in pigtails and a checkered blue dress, ruby slippers, no underwear or bra. She kept twirlin' and liftin' her dress, her titties bouncin' them tiny pink nipples into little hard-ons until she was done spinnin'. Horny Dorothy kept doin' her solo thing until four men in Zoot suits and a woman dressed as June Cleaver carried her to a corner to have their way with her. For the rest of the night, you could hear that girl moaning and screaming. And all I could do was stand there and watch and listen."

"And that's when I introduced myself," Gary says, patting Carol's arm.

"Scared the shit out of me is what you did."

Gary grins. "Yeah, but I made up for it."

"All right, I admit it," Carol says, kissing his hand. "Mr. Trench Coat takes my hand and pulls me out to the dance floor. We sway for a song or two, smoke a little, snort a little, and we just tease each other for the rest of the night. We play little games of switcheroo, go off to dance with other people for a minute or two, kissing and teasing, and then we come back. I already knew who was taking me home—I wanted to wait 'til no one was dancin' anymore. I never wanted anyone as much as I wanted this lug."

"And it wasn't easy," Gary says, adding, "not easy at all. You wouldn't believe what was happening around us. Groups of bodies, daisy chains, rows, piles—pretty much every body was on the business end of somebody doing something. And we kept creepin' to the entrance, stepping over a big Liza Minnelli pile sucking and grinding next to a heap of Shirley Temples lickin' their good clit lollipops. My favorite was this room of Wizard of Oz Munchkins fucking, sucking and pissing on each other as 'Staying Alive' blasted through the speakers. Drew quite a crowd I can tell you."

Carol laughs. "That's when I KNEW it was time to go."

"Good thing too," Gary says. "There was a long row of men jerking off against the wall and shooting their wads in tandem like the fucking Bellagio fountain. I'd had enough too and couldn't wait to leave with Janis Joplin."

"They were aiming at us when we ran by them too," Carol adds. "Oh, y'all have no idea how good it was to get the hell outta there—the smells alone were enough to make you sick as a dog. Thank God we were high and I was dry."

"Why dry?" I ask.

Gary relights his cigar. "My trench coat was probably the wisest costume to wear," he says, dipping the chewed end into his whiskey. "Soon's we got to my pick-up truck, I threw that coat away and drove us back to my shithole apartment butt-ass naked."

"Which was fine by me, kiddies," Carol sings, adding, "'cause I was just as naked as he was the moment I stepped out of the truck. We've been together ever since."

Meghan has her hand in my crotch. With more than a slight slur, she says, "And all that really happened? You're shitting us."

Carol puts her hands up. "True story, as God is my witness."

"Carol tells the best stories," Gary brags. "And that's the tame version of our Meet-Cute love-at-first-blight relationship story. She wrote a totally different version, a wilder, detail-specific hardcore graphic version that Penthouse published."

"No kidding," I say, truly impressed. "Just the one story?"

Carol blushes and shakes her head with a dismissive wave of her hand. "A few more here and there," she says. "It pays the bills."

Gary guffaws. "Pays the bills, she says—this foxy broad has the magic touch," he says with a wide smile. "Joss, you are looking at the head of BLUE Media."

"That crazy successful new porn company? Really?"

BLUE? *Everyone knows about BLUE,* I'm thinking.

"EROTIC, if you don't mind, hubby," Carol says, gently tapping Gary's arm. "This blue-eyed lug spoke out of turn, Jossie-honey, so ignore him. I mean, just because our life is filled with crazy fucking and love-making, he thinks it's all porn."

"Typical male," Meghan says.

Gary guffaws. "Carol's being modest and slightly dishonest because we're still getting to know you," he says, adding, "but she's right, as per usual. I did speak out of turn. I usually don't brag about my woman's erotic empire, but they money it makes is pornographic, I'll tell you that much. Helps keep the ranch going."

"You have a ranch," I say, suddenly wishing I were Gary.

Carol rolls her eyes. "We own a fair bit of land outside of Cherokee," she says, lighting a Virginia Slim, her Southern accent fading to flat and more professional. "Blue Mountain Ranch is our home. It's also a retreat center, a resort and spa, and headquarters of BLUE. As sex therapists and marriage counselors, we use the ranch for our intensive workshops, group therapy and activities, counseling sessions, and intimacy training. Because sex is the main component of our process, we built a massive compound for privacy, which is why our success rate's second to none. BLUE is an extension of the work done there."

Gary makes a sleepy, smarmy smile. "BLUE," he says, nuzzling Carol's ear. "Hands-down the best in the industry, a sapphire in the crown of our careers."

Meghan whispers in my ear loud enough for all to hear. "I'm so horny, Jossie-Joss," she hisses. "I want to suck your cock and fall asleep with it in my mouth."

The fire pops. I look at my sloppy would-be girlfriend. She continues making like a bobble head. I'm not terribly embarrassed, but I am annoyed. I don't mind inebriation with good friends in a private setting, but not in public and never in front of strangers.

Meghan's ideas of propriety haven't changed in the two years we've been apart. Her penchant for drinking too much and making scenes is more than just a big turnoff.

For me, it's close to a deal breaker.

"That was vivid," I say, trying to mask my impatience. Shaking my head, I offer Carol and Gary a pathetic shrug for an apology.

Meghan squeezes my hand, her head wobbling as she pulls away. She laughs herself into hysterics, loud near-braying donkey joy. I press my lips to her ear. "Honey, you've had enough."

She yanks her hand and glares at me. "I'm not your wife," she says, spilling her booze. "Oopsie-daisy. Carol 'n Gary, thanks for sharing that beautiful erotic adventure with me and ol' stick-in-the-mud, Joss—tellin' me I've had enough. You don't have the right to tell me I've had enough. Just 'cause we're fucking doesn't mean we're back together."

With tears in her eyes, Meghan looks at the ice in her glass. "I'm-I'm-I'm had much too-to-to drink, Joss, an' I dinnit mean to say that," she says, her bottom lip quivering before her face suddenly brightens. "So, Gary and Carol, how romantically gross that story was. All I can think about now is stacks of horny little people pissing on and sucking off each other as the Bee Gees sing. It's gross, but kinda hot though. Baby, Jossie, let's go put your junk in my mouth and make you come. I'm sorry I'm sloppy. I know you hate me for it."

With a sigh for Gary and Carol, I pet Meghan's hair. "What makes her horny usually makes me shudder and want to take a hot shower," I tell them.

Carol smiles. "Sounds like you're missing out to me, Joss."

Gary laughs. "There was a shower room too—that night," he says, snapping and turning to Carol. "Tell them about those costumed cowboys."

Carol's accent returns as she says, "Gary-honey, story for another day—yes, Joss?"

"Yeah, I'm good," I say, waving a hand in surrender.

Meghan whispers, "I'm very drunk and need to pee."

Carol puts out her cigarette. "I got this one, Jossie-honey," she says, helping Meghan to her feet. "This might take a while, but I can make soberin' up time into some honest-to-goodness girl talk. You menfolk oughta go outside for some cigars and a big-ass nightcap. Y'all should talk, get to know each other better."

As the women go, Gary says, "That's Carol-speak for don't come back 'til after midnight. Alright, Joss, let's mosey to the patio—we can chat around the fire pit under the stars, mano a mano."

*

I light up a cigarette and heave a heavy sigh.

The night is young and very cold. Thank God I won that karaoke competition a few nights ago—this leather bomber number is an absolute dream coat.

"Some story, Gary," I say, finishing my highball.

"Got that right, bubba," he chuckles, puffing his stogie. "I swear to God there wasn't anything about that crazy place I hadn't seen before or since, and I mean nothing. I'm the only true libertine I know, but for some reason, I have nightmares about that night. Maybe deep in my subconscious, I'm punishing myself for having debased myself to depravity."

I dismiss Gary's libertine comment.

In hindsight, a stupid thing to do, as it might've spared Meghan and me—but I'm getting ahead of myself. At this point, Gary is charming, witty, dashing, playfully brooding, warm, effusive, deeply interested, and intensely engaging.

Come into my parlor, said the libertine spider to the fly.

"Must be the pissing disco midgets," I tell him. "I still have nightmares about seeing my parents fuck each other with strap-on dildos when I was five, but to be fair, it was the last time I ever saw them alive, which might explain why I have nightmares."

A look of concern clouds Gary's face. "Nightmares, among other things, I'm sure—I'm so sorry to hear that, Joss," he says, leaning closer, his hands linked, his elbows on his knees. "I mean that. Losing one parent at an early age is bad enough, but losing them both is tragic—would you mind telling me what happened?"

"Not at all," I say. "But I'd like another drink."

"Ah, yes—we need a big-ass nightcap for discussion of such things," Gary says, whistling to the barkeeper. "Hey, Billy-boy, that bottle of *Aberfeldy 21* and two glasses." He turns back to me with a grin. "Sometimes, you gotta drop some bones if you want the best. We got more cash than we could ever spend in three lifetimes thanks to Carol's business and horse sense. I love that woman and her voodoo money-making magic."

"Gary, you already bought our dinner."

"I'll fuck your propriety in the ass with my big cock," he says with a laugh. "We don't mind sharing our wealth with friends—and I hope we'll be just that, Joss Parker. To you and to Meghan, I hope we'll all be good friends." The sound of his voice is almost a growl. I can't tell if he's being sincere or playing with me, teasing me, maybe even tempting me.

Again, I can only nod.

Billy the Barkeep puts down the two glasses and opens up a hinged orange and black shoe box-sized case. Inside is a squat bottle with a dark, honey-hued liquor. Gary hands the barkeep a $100-dollar bill and tells him to scoot, which makes the young man smile (and blush for some reason).

"How old are you, Joss?"

"Twenty-six," I tell him.

"And what do you do?"

"Temp work, odd jobs," I say, "enough to pay bills and give me time to audition, perform, and write."

After a moment of thought, Gary uncorks the bottle on the table. "Ever had Scotch before?" he asks. "I bet not like this beauty." A deep sniff of the cork before he offers it to me. "That's the fucking stuff, bubba. Fruit and honey, fresh snappy fragrance." He pours us each a glass. He brings his to his nose, closes his eyes, and breathes.

I do the same and feel a little tingle this time.

"What do you smell?" Gary asks. "Don't think."

My eyes still closed, I tell him, "Vanilla, oak, smoke, and honey."

"That's a good nose, bubba—have a taste now, and roll it around the inside of your mouth for a bit," he says, softly. "Over the teeth, under the lips, the front and back of your tongue. Let it ease and trickle slowly down your throat, and feel the burn warming you all the way to your crotch."

"You're making it sound like sex, Gary."

He smiles. "Because it is, Joss," he says, savoring another sip. "People experience the world using one or two senses at a time usually—wouldn't you say that's true?"

"Sure, I guess."

"Is that how you like to fuck too?"

It's more than a blunt question—it's loaded and leading, but I'm curious. "Do I really have to answer that?" I tell him.

Gary laughs. "Great, mind-blowing sex requires the use all the senses in order to fully appreciate the experience," he says. "Which is why I prefer to experience all of life in the same way. Using all your senses opens you to the idea of exploring opportunities to their fullest potential—why can't your exploration be sexual? Now, describe the Scotch."

I breathe the vapors again and take a sip. I savor the taste as Gary suggested and swallow, breathing deep as it goes down in the long slow burn. "Oak and vanilla," I tell him, opening my eyes. "Musk, salt and caramel, spicy licorice, dry at the finish, warm. It's fucking fantastic."

This time he winks. "Indeed it is, my dear boy—new things usually are when you let yourself go balls deep into the unknown." He refills our glasses. "We got sidetracked—tell me what happened to your parents."

Lighting a cigarette, I say, "I went to school that next morning and they went to work—they drove into the city together. They didn't come home. Car crash, head on. It was some truck driver going the wrong way. That's Atlanta highways for you."

Gary thinks for a moment. "Any brothers, sisters? Family?"

"Nope, I'm all orphan," I tell him, adding, "like Meghan."

"Is she now?"

"Yeah, I first met her when I was young, but then I didn't see her again until we were teenagers," I tell him, blowing smoke. "We met again after college—she's been in theater forever. I happened to see a new play she was doing, and we started dating casually. I got serious, she wasn't ready. Then I wasn't ready when she was. We broke up, got back together, fell in and out of love with other people, and did it again. Falling in love at the same time was a nice surprise—but of course, we still broke up in the end. I didn't see her for several months, but we got back together, as per usual.

"I moved back in, things were fine for a month or two, and then she started prancing around Atlanta like the Whore of Babylon, an insatiable psychopathic slut. She was off the chain too. Thank God she didn't get herpes or HIV or hep C. Still, we couldn't make it work, so I left."

Gary sighs. "Jesus, Joss—how long ago was that?"

"Two years," I reply. "Last week, she calls me out of the blue and says she wants to try again. I nearly told her to fuck off for the rest of my life. I've never been good at telling her no. So, we take a week off for a trip on the Blue Ridge Parkway to rekindle and possibly reconnect."

"You're not technically together then."

"No, we're not," I tell him. "Being with her feels the same in some ways. It also feels forced and hollow. She's holding back, and I'm holding back. If we have a real chance then I'm having a hard time seeing it."

"What don't you see, Joss?"

I give Gary a shrug. "I don't know. You can't go back though, can you? I mean, not really. We're different people now, our lives are different now. Maybe we need someone to help us through this."

Gary clears his throat. "Joss, I'm a fucking therapist," he says, swirling the Scotch in his glass. "And right now, I might be able to help you."

"It's also an amazing coincidence," I tell him.

"Indeed it is," Gary says with a smile. "You two fight a lot when you were a couple?"

"No, we didn't talk to each other—we broke up a lot," I tell him, feeling my buzz loosen my tongue. "That's our relationship: we fuck a lot, we love each other deeply, but we don't talk about important things. We hide things, we're both insecure, we're scared to lose each other but do things to hurt each other, you know?"

"Which is what exactly, Joss?" Gary asks. "I won't judge, bubba—I can see you need to talk about what's eating you. Maybe I can help."

That's when I spill the rest of it.

All the words, the emotions, the fears, the regrets—the chain of events leading to each break up and each reunion. The lies I tell her, the lies she tells me, the secrets we both keep—the anger, the resentment. I've talked to Gary for over an hour before I realize most of the patrons outside were gone.

"Fuck me, man," I say, noting the time on the clock behind him. "It's almost midnight. I vomited in your lap. I'm sorry."

Gary laughs. "I told you to talk to me," he says. "I do this for a living, and I think Carol and I can help you guys, Joss. Chances are good that Carol got Meghan sobered up enough to get her to talk to her. Maybe we can help you two get to the right path."

Whatever that path may be.

"Thanks, Gary," I tell him, raising my glass. "To new friends."

He raises his glass. "New friends," he says, drinking. "Listen, what we do as therapists is unique. We're unconventional people—we're unconventional therapists. The results speak for themselves—the testimonials of the couples we help would fill volumes. I mean, Carol is the CEO of BLUE because of our success, for fuck's sake. It's mad, that is."

"Why is it mad?"

"Our techniques employ sex as the key component to the therapy—thank GOD for the walls around our place," he says with a laugh. "What sometimes goes on in there isn't for the faint of heart or the uninitiated. What we do is risqué, from sex surrogacy to small and large group masturbation to communal air bathing to creative classes in erotic arts—learning to perform, write, film, stage, and even market what you envision."

"What if your vision is fucked-up?"

"There is evil in the world, and predators have no place in our center," he replies, with utter seriousness. "We've learned how to weed out the psychopaths from the committed couples, the ones who want to work through their individual issues as couples."

"And you do it through sex," I say.

"We offer week-long, month-long, and year-long programs because wrangling sexuality can be quite nuclear—it takes time to get a handle on its power," Gary explains. "We assess each couple, as each couple has its own set of desires, fears, needs, and goals, and we build a unique program for them. That being said, no couple is an island—each one forms an archipelago. Separate but connected facilitates better results."

"Do you think there's hope for us?"

"There's always hope, whether separately or together, hope is always there," Gary says, rather cryptically. "Comes down to how willing you are to face your pain together and then share that bond for life. Some don't want that kind of shared history and part ways."

"I don't follow."

Gary thinks for a moment. "People who say they have a history together are usually implying some shared experience they faced together," he says. "Power in communion of what you both experience. Soldiers and the burden of war. Police officers and fire fighters and the crime and fires they face. They share the same experiences, and understand each other through what they experience together. Extreme examples. Non-life threatening events can be traumatic experiences the first time. Those can hit children like bricks."

"Holy shit," I tell him, thinking of my own childhood.

Gary nods. "So, when a couple comes to us for treatment, first we help them pinpoint those early issues. Then we help them bond using our unconventional program. As they sift through their pasts as a couple, they forge a new intimacy. Then we make them share their struggles and victories publicly and sexually, which is so terrifying that the experiences bind them as if they were soldiers entrenched in a foxhole. Our couples remake broken relationships into something resilient and life-lasting," he says. "It takes hard work and time and patience. Like any therapy tool, it's only as effective as what you put into it."

Suddenly, I feel like he's selling me something, and yet, the promise of it makes me tremble. Like Carol and Gary the magic couple, this perfectly well adjusted and successful couple, the promise of not losing Meghan seems too good to be true. Not to mention fucking expensive. I mean a private retreat can't be cheap.

And when you don't know what it's like to order a $300 bottle of Scotch and then tip a $100 on top of that, it sounds even more expensive.

Hope stirs, if only for a moment, and then fades back to reality.

I'm just grateful to Gary for listening to me whine about my relationship. He's so patient too, sitting across from me waiting for me as I process this.

Waiting for me to tell him that he sold me on his pitch.

Gary claps his hands. "Listen, here's what I'm gonna do—what you both need most is a hard-hitting crash course in forgiveness," he says, looking at his watch. "It's not late for me, and I'm sure Carol will have some insight after we talk. We won't charge you a dime either. We just got back from a conference in Winston-Salem, and we have some materials we can put together for you to peruse tomorrow. Some exercises, some naughty stories, some case studies, some challenges. We'll meet you at your hotel in Cherokee tomorrow night." That sucks all the wind from my lungs.

Would Meghan want to try something like this?

Would I want to?

Gary stretches. "You make the rules for your relationship," he says. "You create your world and make it go round. Carol and I went through hell before we were finally able to do that. I hit her once. She stabbed me twice. She cheated on me. I cheated on her. She likes women more than she does men, but I love her and she loves me. I like women and men, but she loves me and I love her. When we learned to let go and forgive each other and ourselves, we found a deeper love and a much stronger bond through our sexuality. We opened it up beyond the confines of traditional marriage and became who we are."

"And that's the secret? An open marriage?"

"No, my dear boy, forgiveness is the secret, and also the first step," he replies. "Sex is the one thing that can create or destroy in a relationship, but forgiveness comes first."

I don't tell him how I really feel about that.

There's something logical and yet dangerously taboo about this 'pitch'. But I have to start somewhere, and I do love Meghan. The fire pit ashes rise in the pine-scented air as I finish the Scotch, savoring the smoky sweet liquor burning my throat with oaky spice, earthy vanilla, and heat.

"What should I do?"

Gary leans forward. His darkly handsome face and gray eyes

pierce my returning gaze. He sips the last bit of liquor from his glass and smiles. "Come on now, Joss—you know what you need to do," he says. "You think you don't, but you do."

"Gary, I'm not gay."

He laughs. "Joss, my dear boy, drop the defensive macho man routine," he says. "Do you want Meghan in your life or not? Do you want a bond that cleaves her to you, and you to her, as if, from Holy Writ, it were a sacred covenant?"

"Yes."

Do I mean that?

"What would you sacrifice for that?"

"Anything."

Do I mean that?

Gary reaches into his jacket pocket and fishes out a small book. "Read this tonight, and then ask yourself this question," he says. "Would you allow yourself to be swallowed by the whale, like Jonah did, and return from the belly of the beast like a man reborn?"

*

Meghan is not in our room.

A note from Carol says she's staying with them and that they'll bring her back tomorrow morning with breakfast. I'm relieved, to tell you the truth. I've had a strange enough night without me having to play nursemaid to a drunk for the rest of it.

Besides, I have a homework assignment from Gary Rider. I toss his book of mystery on the dresser and get ready for bed.

After a shower and thorough mouth brushing, I settle in for a night alone, feeling tinges of guilt for not wanting to sleep with Meghan tonight.

"Christ, I'm tired," I say to myself, rubbing my eyes.

The soft cover book fits into my hand. There's a title in gold letters, but it's too faded and in French.

When I open it up, I'm not surprised to see small writing on its thin pages. I chuckle as I picture Gary as a communist trying to push his Marxist ideology through one of Chairman Mao's little red cookbooks. What I find on these pages, however, are from a wholly different philosophy.

> *All are a part of Nature; when she created men, she was pleased to vary their tastes as she made different their countenances, and we ought no more be astonished at the diversity she has put in our features than at that she has placed in our affections.*

I am too tired from the whiskey to keep my eyes open. I manage one more passage before finally succumbing to sleep.

*

The Folder

> *The piece of me you eat, taking to face,*
> *Forcing my vision and periphery*
> *Toward the montage of our coupled grace.*
> *I can't but weep from this, our ecstasy.*
>
> —Simone Simon, from *Precipice*

THE NEXT MORNING, GARY AND CAROL STOP BY THE ROOM. They bring breakfast for four, as well as my missing companion. Soon, we're sitting in the little nook by the window making small talk about plans for the rest of the trip to Cherokee.

The room gets a little stuffy, so I open one of the large windows. A cold wind catches Meghan's hair and musses it over her face. We all laugh as she spits strands caked with grits.

A half hour later, we're packed and ready to go. It's time to say our goodbyes. Carol (wearing an electric-blue jumpsuit) takes our hands and sits with us on the bed.

Gary (in matching jumpsuit) hands me a manila folder (in exchange for the book I didn't read). "Everything you need is in the folder," he says, pocketing the book. "It'll tell you what to do in what order."

"We hand-selected the material to inspire some real conversation between y'all," Carol adds, her excitement bubbly. "Should ignite some real fire in your loins too—oh, my Jesus Wept."

Gary nods. "Look, there's nothing in the world like fucking—but fucking from one end of the Parkway to the other won't fix you. Talking is the only thing that will, so talk to each other. Today. Right now."

"That simple?" Meghan asks, wiping a tear.

Carol smiles. "That simple, honey," she says in her drawl. Turning to me, she adds, "No fucking on the way, you hear me, buckshot? And you call as soon as you get to the hotel. By then, you'll either be on the road to forever or ready to close up shop with a little more love and respect for each other. You win either way, but we can help y'all get right with movin' on. The back and forth together and apart stops today, kids."

"It's just fear," Gary says, gently. "So, talk about your fear."

"Fear of what?" I ask.

Carol smiles. "That's for y'all to figure out. I'm not a psychic, although my intuition is as sharp as a knife," she says, hugging Meghan and then me. "No fuckin'—just talking and listening. Y'all might have a hard time with my 'no fucking' rule, what with all the stuff we put in that folder, but it's important y'all don't."

Gary smiles. "Try to remember we're good at what we do," he says. "We have your best interests in mind, as individuals and as a couple. For you two, fucking means not facing the truth."

No, that didn't sound menacing at all.

What are you not telling us, McDude?

Carol begins to tear up. "Y'all be careful on the Parkway—it's supposed to rain all afternoon," she says, kissing my cheek. "We'll see y'all in a few hours."

Gary kisses Meghan and extends his hand to me. As I shake it, his gaze doesn't waver. His gray eyes remind me that he knows me my secrets. My heart is pounding by the time he and Carol leave. I'm scared and excited, confused and nervous, and while I do look forward to the drive on the Parkway, I can't stop wondering whether the Riders are who they say they are and what they seem to be.

*

After warming up the car, leaving the parking lot, filling up with gas at a nearby station, we start the last leg of our trip. Once again, we move slowly along the serpentine artery of the Blue Ridge Parkway. One more day, one more night, one more chance to salvage us. Past and future collides into the present again.

We wend our way through parked cars and fog.

Holding hands, our grasped fingers intertwine like fleshy weaves of desperate affection. Deciding whether we should forge ahead with our reunion makes the looming hours of the day frightening. Here we break new ground. Here we put things to rest. Deciphering the truths buried in our separate catacombs of regret and insecurity, of guilt and selfishness, of seething hatred for one another's weaknesses—discovery is why we're here.

What should we discuss then? I don't know. Gary and Carol seem to know something we don't know, and they don't even know us. Time ticks softly, easily, sweetly. No secrets uttered as of yet.

Yes, let's pretend we have nothing to hide.

Meghan kisses my cheek. "I'm sorry about last night—I shouldn't have had that last brandy," she says, adding, "and Carol insisted I sleep it off after we talked. I hope you didn't mind me staying out."

"It was kind of nice having the big bed to myself for one night."

"I'll make up for last night when we get to Cherokee," she purrs in my ear. "Let's open the folder."

"I guess we should," I tell her, "but I need to whet my whistle."

Meghan giggles. "You're a dork for saying that," she says, "but I think you're swell."

We pull into a car-packed, people-cramped, tucked-away folk art center. The niche of the Parkway has little signs darting to and fro across paths adjacent to the road. Not very noticeable, as they are foliage colored. The center is for tourists and boasts of having relics of sacred Indian lands and genuine stones grafted from the Smoky Mountains and other authentic bric-a-brac.

I park slightly askew between two enormous white lines littered with pine straw and gravel and some browning leaves newly tossed from over-hanging oaks.

Good enough, I tell myself.

The frosty wind from Asheville is still with us. Its misty chill makes me shudder as I grab Meghan's hand and walk to the large log cabin. Its bucolic facade belies the clandestine tourist traps inside. We climb the stoop, mountain folk music wafting from hidden speakers behind the rows of rocking chairs on the porch.

"Nice jacket, baby," Meghan tells me, pinching my ass as we open the door.

Later, after we've rummaged and pilfered the racks and bins, I buy my best gal an authentic Indian-crafted scarf and mitten set. For myself, I buy sodas and bottles of water. We leave the log cabin store in silence, our words caged inside our hearts.

What are we afraid of? I don't know.

As we walk together, uncertain of the future and situated in the past, we seek solace in familiar silence instead of the hope of illumination and possibility. But the uncertainties—I feel like we're under siege, everything is so fucking fragile right now. Anything could shatter us into a thousand pieces. What Gary said about fucking being great but hollow without communication—he's right.

Since Meghan and I are still not talking, I think about the fucking. I need something to hold onto until one of us tries to break the wall. Apparently, so does Meghan, as I feel her hand on the front of my jeans as we walk with our bag of winter garb and sundries. She's walking ahead of me, so she stops and rubs my crotch when I bump into her. She turns around and kisses me before we resume our stroll back to the car. She takes the scarf and mittens out of the bag and smiles. "Just like the Indians made in the olden timey days," she says, putting them on. "See? I'm Pocahontas."

The scarf is a mass of gaudy colors. The wool is thick and hairy.

"I was gonna say the same thing," I tell her.

And I smile as I watch the colors of the scarf reflect on the tender ticklish flesh under her chin. Turquoise, amber, ebony, yellow ochre, burnt sienna, copper, crimson—colors exotic and foreign, and hinted with blue. Though wet and cold, the spirits of the wind and the trees suddenly make magical the silence I'd feared.

Of course, the fear will return. In droves.

We get in the car. Meghan opens the folder and flips through the pages, inspects them. "There's a CD in the back with a note from Gary and Carol," she says, sliding the disc into my player. "It says to play this first and that there are other tracks to play in turn."

*

Carol's Voice:

"Y'all make the rules for your life together. So long as your rules don't kill somebody, there are no limits. Having a companion and being in a committed relationship are not necessarily equal, but they're not mutually exclusive either. Gary and I want to give you a chance to decide what is best for you and for each other."

Gary's Voice:

"The older I get, the more I see a universe that makes more sense when I participate in its infinity and not its limits. Living is a process of discovery and failure. Nothing is certain. Nothing is fixed. Everything is flawed and imperfect. Life can be tragic, sublime, or boring—but most of that is up to you. You can live in fear or live in wonder, but for fuck's sake, pick one and do it. Pick a path and go. Don't tip toe, just go. If you fuck up, then start over. Remember, we're all food for worms. We only have a brief moment to experience this lucid dream of life, so quit your bitching and talk to each other. That's it. Find the courage and talk."

Carol's Voice:

"Now, before y'all dive into the folder, I want each of you to tell the other something that isn't easy or pleasant to say. Find an overlook, sit on a bench, and spill your secrets, anything you've hidden from one another. Confess to some sin you committed or a shame you've carried for too long. Don't hold back on the ugly either. Truth can be a bitter pill to swallow, but when the goal is forgiveness, it's worth it. See y'all in Cherokee—be brave, be honest, let go, and let God. Amen, kiddies—amen!"

*

I spy a picnic table perfectly hidden in the trees. There seems to be some bits of light breaking the misty sky. It may not last long, so

I suggest we go sit at the observation ledge there. "GPS says a walking trail goes down to a waterfall," I offer, my heart beating like a wild thing. "If you want to go."

From the car, we scramble over felled bits of tree and rolling rock to reach the tiny little clearing. Looking snugly and warm in her mittens and scarf, Meghan sits on the bench.

"So, we tell the truth," she says.

"I guess so," I reply. "We're lying to each other if we think this trip will solve our problems, baby. You know it. I know it."

"So, then I'll go first," she says.

Silence, like a gloved hand. I feel the it wrap slowly, tightly around my reddened neck. I wonder what lie she'll go with first, what horrible transgression. I wonder what I'll confess.

Fuck, I have so many sins.

There is a distant roar of falling water below us. It is a comforting sound, and I think of it as a sign that perhaps, we are purging the bad karma, what we've done to each other in the past that brought us here. Birds flutter above us. The sun peeks through the gloom, as the view becomes a spectacular one. The sky brightens above the trees, perfect for the first incision. A wind blows, and Meghan looks at me, her blue eyes on the brink of tears.

She takes my hand and pulls me next to her.

And finally, it comes out.

"You already know this, but I need to say it," Meghan says. "I cheated on you, all the time. And you think you know why, you-

you think it was because I wanted to get back at you for loving me, to get back at you for taking me back every time, to get back at my father for abusing my sister and me, to get back at my mother for letting him. Maybe all of that is true, Joss, but when it comes down to it, I know I'm different. Cheating on you opened a Pandora's Box for me," she says in a weird whisper. "I loved hurting you because it got me off. And I fantasized about you punishing me for it. You never did, which drove me crazy. It threw me back and forth between loving you more and wanting to hurt you more. You don't know how many times I fucked around on you. Secret hookups in bathroom stalls at work, highway rest stops, gym locker rooms, old houses and churches, mausoleums, and—"

"Meghan, I knew what you were doing," I interrupt. "And I knew it turned you on. But I loved you and just accepted it. I followed you whenever I could manage it."

"You did?"

I smile and shrug. "It was a turn on for me," I confess. "It took awhile, but I enjoyed watching you with other men. I loved watching you with women even more, but you really loved letting those boys give it to you."

"I wish you would've told me," she says.

"You would've stopped," I say, "and I didn't want you to stop. It made sex with you better."

"I would've stopped," she admits, looking at my hands. "But you left me anyway."

"Yes, I did."

"Why?"

I take a deep breath. "The last time I followed you to a barn the weekend you said you were going to visit your mom. All that Saturday night, I watched you and that artist fuck in that barn. What you two did turned me on more than ever," I admit to her. "I mean, come on, he had all those canvases laid out on the floor with those buckets of paint opened between them. And for hours, you fucked in the wet paint, brushed your naked bodies with all those different colors, and rolled around the canvases."

Meghan blushes. "It was pretty hot, wasn't it?"

I nod. "Yeah, it was but not because of you, but because of Ben."

Meghan looks at me. "You knew his name was Ben?"

"Yes, I did."

So, here's my confession: "Because I spent a whole week with him in that barn doing the same thing back when we had graduated from college, Meghan," I tell her. "He said he fell in love with me, but I couldn't say the same thing. You know me, Meghan—I'm kinky, but I'm not gay. I told Ben as much before I left. I never saw him until that night you and he were rolling in the deep. I left after you told him you loved him."

"You heard that?"

"I did, and it pissed me off, so I left," I told her. "I guess I was pissed for lots of reasons, but mainly for that. Was it a lie? Did you fall in love with him?"

She turns her face. "I'm not sure," she replies, "but maybe I did for a few days. I mean he brought out something inside me that was beautiful, something no one else ever did for me. Why would I not love him for it? Ben told me we were making self-portraits, and that mine were real art. He said he'd hang one of them in his gallery. I wonder if he ever did."

He never did, but I'm not ready to tell Meghan why.

I still can't believe I told her about Ben—well, a half-truth about him anyway.

Meghan laughs. "I guess when you're fucking most of the men in Cobb County, you're bound to fuck one of the guys your boyfriend did too, huh?"

She's pissed now—I can see the jealousy.

"Of course, you fucked Ben—you're hot, he's hot, why not? Is he why you left me, Joss? Is it because I cheated on you with your ex-boyfriend and you were jealous? God, I hope so—I hope it tore you to pieces. It must have, Joss, because you left that weekend before I even came home. Out of the dozens of men and women I fucked, you never left—fate took a hand and connected me with a blast from your past, and you bolt."

"Shut-up, Meghan."

"Did you secretly love dear Benny, Joss? Is that what it is? You always loved him and were too much of a pussy to admit it? I mean, you could've jumped down from the rafters to join us, you fucking pussy. Holy fuck, you didn't do a goddamn thing but go home with your limp dick between your legs, punch out our bedroom window, and vanish. No note, no warning, no return address, nothing. You fell off the face of the earth. Would you have gotten in touch with me had we not bumped into each other downtown a year later?"

For a brief moment, I'm furious. But then she turns her face and starts to giggle, which becomes a laugh that gets out of control. Then we're both laughing and it reconnects us, makes us feel less hurt. Because we're both hurt and fearful of all the truths that we began to flay. We retreat and live to lie another day.

"Look, any time you want to have a threesome, Joss, you tell me next time," she says. "I don't want to punish you for loving me anymore."

"You need a nap," I say to lighten the mood. "You're a bitch when you're overtired."

She smiles. "That day you left I sat on the edge of our bed for sixteen hours straight. I didn't move, and I pissed where I sat, not bothering to clean myself. I cried myself to sleep in pissy panties and sheets. When I woke the next day, you weren't there holding me, like I hoped you'd be—I grew desperate after that."

"What do you mean?"

Meghan shrugs. "There were things I had to do to forget you," she says, looking away. "Things you might not like when I tell you. Maybe I won't tell you. Or maybe I will when we see Gary and Carol again. For now, tell me something to make me feel like I'm not a bitchy cunt. Tell me something good."

There is only one thing I want to tell her, and I doubt it's the something good she wants to hear. The reason Ben never showed her paintings was because I bought them all.

I have them in storage.

I want to tell her about a poem I wrote about the night I watched her and Ben, that I'd left it for her in her mailbox a week later and took it out the next day, that I want to recite it for her and can't find the courage.

she hit me with her self-portrait
marred with blackened blood
and resented my own weakness—

she hit me with her night desires—
plain, disintegrated lullabies
dripping with her melancholy

she hit me with her beauty
and scarred me for my sanity.
now I wake in darkness, cold

and shaking in wont for warmth
she stabbed me with her blush
her pouty rose colored lips

her dirty-soled, paint-stained feet
she hit me with her self-portrait
and made me see the truth—

that love is pitch, not pink
she hit me with fear
she hit me with her,
and now am I imprinted
in her likeness.

I do that, if I open up a vein with that poem, it'll only lead us back to talk of Ben. That can and must wait until later. And I'm not ready to open my veins for her.

Not yet.

After all, what's talk compared to this silence. I take a deep breath and then her hand. I don't say anything else—*what can I possibly say now?*

We gaze at one another, and in that silence, I somehow find my courage to speak the volumes I never could before.

Gary might tell me to nut up or shut up. Carol might say something akin to it, but with that sexy drawl. For a moment, only in my mind, I tell them to butt the fuck out of my business and let me be my own goddamn man.

I'm not a coward—*I am not.*

"Meghan, I don't know if what I'm going to say is good or bad—Gary might tell me it's still fucking and not deep talking," I begin, sighing because I don't know where I'm going with this. "I don't care what he thinks right now."

"So just say it, Joss."

"Do you know what it's like for me when I'm inside you? It's a religious experience. I am worshiping you through the center of you. I am totally devoted, riveted, driven mad with ecstasy like Saint Teresa. Your pussy has enslaved me. It's there I find the love I need, crave and desire. Tell me what is a better way to win a man's heart—please, I want to know the answer because for me, no amount of talking compares. From your pussy, I must take my holy sacrament, to drink of your blood and taste of your body, to discover the god in me through my devotion to the goddess in you. Yours is the center of creation, the cradle of my civilization, and for this, I am bound only to you."

There is so much more I want to say, but I suddenly feel embarrassed and vulnerable, and so, I remain silent. Suddenly, her mouth is on my mouth.

A tongue darting inside, pulling mine into her mouth. Hard kiss like steel and iron. A kiss filled with power and fire. A blue kiss. A kiss of deep blue. A kiss of even deeper blue turned red.

Slowing down, her lips soften to down, her mouth feminine and pliant. I taste her sweet salt.

I taste her tears.

"I'm sorry," she whispers, her voice fading into the rippling shush of pines swaying in the cold mountain breezes. "We should do this without all the tears though. Oh, how I wish we could do this without all the tears."

And then we're back in the car taking the winding mountain

pass. I'm lost in the smell of her perfume, the scent of her skin and hair. My crotch twitches and jumps from suddenly wanting her, needing her.

It's a distraction, I know, because deep down I know what's coming for us after we start pushing through the pain.

I know what's waiting for us on the other side of these truths. The truths of our doom, I fear, are self-evident. I'm fooling myself if I don't acknowledge Sherman's Second March to the Sea.

And I wonder who will burn this time.

*

Remaking Love

In time, perhaps, our lucid dreams shall wake
Our one desire to name this love we make.

—Simone Simon, from *Precipice*

WE DRIVE FOR AN HOUR IN SILENCE. Meghan suddenly clears her throat. "The note in the folder says we should play the next track on the CD before reading the first set of pages," she says. "It also talks about there being more power in the sense of hearing than many people believe. And then there's a quote that Gary scribbled down."

"What quote?"

Meghan chuckles. "From the Marquis de Sade," she says, scrunching her shoulders. "He's a naughty bastard—I'll try to read Gary's chicken scratch. 'If thus the paths conducting the one to virtue and the other to vice are equally bestrewn with briars, why do we not consult Nature and loyally observe her directives? For very few is life a bed of roses. Heed me, and you'll be one who, with the thorns that are there, finds a goodly number of flowers.' The Marquis de Sade believed nature demands her children to fuck like minks," she continues with a happy sigh. "Sounds nice."

"That's odd," I tell her. "It sounds like something Gary was telling me last night, as we imbibed our expensive highland libation," I say, not mentioning the book I neglected to finish reading. "Okay, hit play. Let's listen to some nice vice."

*

Carol's Voice:

"I hope y'all got through the first exercise—if you haven't murdered each other, then it's a good sign that you're on the right path. Time for something less painful. I put one of our first successful test cases on this CD—it's the next track. It's an example of our 'Remaking' technique for bonding couples. A former guest had a painful memory about the day she lost her virginity—it's fairly common, as y'all might imagine. While the experience for her, in and of itself, wasn't that traumatic, the guilt and shame she felt about it affected her for many years, preventing her from enjoying sex with every man afterward, including her new husband. After a few sessions with us, she and her husband worked to remake her painful memory into something positive, something that became a fun, sexy fantasy for them too. Before she and her husband graduated from our program, they reenacted it before a live audience, an intimate performance for the group to enjoy and share with them."

Gary's Voice:

"It's an older recording from an analog audio reel, so the quality isn't all that great. It's still pretty hot—I don't doubt it'll get one or both of you a little warm. The woman's name is Betsy, who was fifty-three when she and her husband did this."

Carol's Voice:

"When Betsy and her husband Leslie first came to us, neither one could gaze into the other's eyes. And they certainly couldn't describe their sexual activities in any detail, let alone with sex-talk words."

Gary's Voice:

"As you'll hear, Betsy and Leslie succeeded beautifully—they're a testament to our remaking love therapy sessions."

*

I was still a virgin the summer I turned seventeen. Casey lived down the block from my parents' beach house in Pensacola, Florida. The days were a mixture of balmy and rainy back then, but every day was a beach day in the summer. I met Casey on the beach one cloudy afternoon.

My parents rarely went to the beach house in those days so I could escape and have little care about life outside of the beach. Casey was thirty, unemployed but independently wealthy. He owned his beach house, and the long strip of land that surrounded it. I liked to jog along the edge of the water there, feeling the sand and the warmth of the tide.

It was there that I saw Casey cloud bathing one afternoon. He was naked and grinning when I passed by gawking at him.

I nearly went tumbling in the surf for my trouble. Boys my own age did nothing for me, so I fantasized about men like Starsky and Hutch having their way with me.

But Casey was no television star. He was a pervert and didn't care who knew it, and I found that intensely erotic.

There he was, sitting on his towel and rolling his cock in his hands. With a wave, he invited me up the dune to watch him finish. I ran to the base of the steps and stood there until a stream of white shot from his penis onto the sand behind his head.

He laughed.

His eyes were closed. Still stroking, he told me to come back again later, that he would show me something better.

The next morning, I debated whether to go. I felt threatened, but I was also excited (and stupidly naive). The thought of Casey stroking himself excited me more than my fantasy of being fondled by a shirtless Shaun Cassidy in a cowboy hat. I wanted to see him pleasure himself again. And I wanted to touch myself as he did it.

I found my courage to go back for another peek. He wasn't in the same spot as the last time, which was out in the open atop the dune. I went up the steps to the fence. I heard a voice calling me from the patio beyond the gate. My heart pounded as I lifted the latch and went inside. I could hear disco playing on the stereo.

A television set with the volume off was there, but I couldn't see the picture. Casey wore a half-closed bathrobe and invited me in. He was a little taller than me. He was lean, had a mustache, and his skin tanned a deep bronze. On the television were three women sucking a man's hard penis.

I mumbled something about never having seen this on network TV before, he laughed and told me it was a video playing from a tape inside the huge bulky block in the counter. He called it a VCR and said it was one of the first in the world. He bragged that he could get anything on tape, including porn films.

I stared at the scene for ten minutes. He stood there beside me watching. We said nothing. I didn't know I was damp between my legs until the guy's semen spurted all over the faces of the three girls.

Casey put his hand on my rump.

Suddenly, he tore my shorts and shirt, taking them off in a ripping motion. He unhooked my bra, pulled off my panties. I was standing only in my socks and running shoes. My breasts were bouncing, and I moaned as his mouth found each of my nipples. His hands felt so different on my breasts than my own did.

Then he opened and dropped his robe to the floor. His cock was erect and shiny. He told me to turn around – I did. As my shorts and panties were pulled down to my ankles, I felt his fingers spread my rear, exposing my virgin flower. He was not gentle as he probed me with his finger. It felt good and painful at the same time.

My juices were stirring, and when he knelt behind me, removing his digit to part my bare cheeks, they flowed. He tasted my rosebud and slipped a finger into my pussy. He said nothing as he got to his feet and shoved his prick inside me. I felt skin pull and stretch, my liquids mingled with blood. It hurt and yet it didn't hurt, but I wanted it over. It hurt and I wanted him to finish.

And I didn't want him to finish.

As he quickened his pace, he began to groan, his hands gripping my waist as he pumped me with abandon. It hurt more than I expected or imagined. It felt good, but I wanted him to finish.

And I didn't want him to finish.

Suddenly, Casey screamed, jerking as he emptied into me. I screamed because it hurt me, but it didn't hurt me. He patted my ass and told me I could use the shower outside to clean off the blood and cum as he walked into some back room in his condo. I picked up my torn clothes and went outside.

```
From a pile of freshly dried laundry, I
grabbed a T-shirt after I showered off and
cleaned my swollen vagina. I went home and
never saw him again.
```

*

Gary's Voice:

"I'm sure you heard the noises in the background. The audio was pre-recorded, which allowed us to use it as the soundtrack for their live performance—her husband played the part of Casey. Many couples found this to be so erotic they participated from their seats."

Carol's Voice:

"Thank the Lord too! What they did led me to my own breakthrough, allowing me to talk candidly about Thomas, who meant something more to me than I knew. We opened up so many doors—we deepened our bond because we didn't hide our feelings about the impacts of others in on our lives. That you are changed because of something other than your current partner often raises problems in relationships."

Gary's Voice:

"In your folder, you'll find a set of pages with a pink paperclip. This story was taken from another couple's virginity-losing experience later that evening. They were so inspired by Betsy and Leslie's performance they developed an erotic short story we later published in one of our first issues of BLUE Magazine. They worked through their pasts together, without us prompting them, and it remade their relationship. Their end-result is meant to inspire you and get you excited about being with us tonight. Remember, no fucking until AFTER you get to the hotel. We're looking forward to seeing you two."

*

Thomas liked boys AND girls, which I found sexy. His mother was my dance instructor at the Pensacola Beach Summer Dance Camp. Thomas was my dance partner because we complemented each other perfectly – his strength, my form. I had a huge crush on him, but never suspected he was crushing on me.

I thought he was gay. It was just an assumption on my part – I was wrong about his true preference.

He later told me it was both.

"Why limit yourself to one kind of pleasure?" he said to me. "The male and female forms can combine in myriad sexy ways, so I prefer to play with both equally."

Thomas was tall, broad-shouldered, smelled like Egyptian musk, and wore a beautifully chiseled face. I assumed he was more inclined to putt from the rough just for having that chin.

The night of our last performance that summer, he and I had a picnic on the beach. We were well into our six-pack of beer when he asked, "Would you consider fucking me?"

I choked on my beer. "To the point, huh, Thomas?"

"I'm curious." He paused. "Would you?"

"Thom, you're a fox and all, but – "

Taking another swig of beer, he said, "C'mon, I want to do something for you. I hate that your first time was with that asshole Casey Wealthy Britches. You deserve better."

"Wait, I thought you were, you know."

"Gay? Only sometimes – boys are a hobby, but women are a dream job."

"Oh, really?"

"Really," he said, putting his beer down. "I want to do something for you."

"You're drunk, you're kinda gay if not all the way gay, and you'll never speak to me again if we have sex, or – what are you doing? Oh, God."

"I'm not drunk, Carol – I'm buzzed, sure, but I want you. Here, stand up."

"On the beach? Right now?"

"Sure, why not? No one ever comes down here this time of night. Just close your eyes and let me be your partner, Carol. We're only dancing. Remember that."

From the small transistor radio at our feet, Dr. Hook started singing about spending the night together, which was one of my favorite songs ever.

I shrugged and closed my eyes with a sigh. "So, we're just dancing then."

Thomas was running his hands down the sides of my arms. I smelled beer on his breath, subtly sweet, almost perfumed, like his sweat. The lights in the studio were dim and moody, naughty if not romantic. He didn't move. He stared at me, caressing my neck and shoulders now, waiting for me to answer him.

I was struggling to make sense of the situation the longer I delayed my decision. It was hard to think, what with the explosion of goose flesh all over my skin and the tingling electric pulse on the lips of my pussy. "I want you, Carol," he whispered.

"Why?"

His hands still barely touching my skin, he slowly leaned into me and traced my cheek and jaw and the soft flesh of my neck with his lips and warm breath. The electricity in my pussy, each tiny shock of plasma, suddenly spiraled inward as waves of heat, coaxing sweat to bead and pools to fill.

A thousand mouths and tongues, thousands of tiny wet openings and probes, cover my body in microscopic kissing from aft to stern. I am powerless.

"What do you want?"

"To make it with you, Carol."

"But--"

Thomas sank to his knees, bit the strings of my shorts, and pulled them loose, the soft fabric bunching at my ankles in a single drop. The panties he pulled with his lips, and this he did so deftly, so quickly, that I was shivering and cold for a half-breath, as his mouth found my other wetter, hotter mouth.

I opened my eyes.

I had no idea what was happening, how it was happening, why it was happening – I let it happen. And I praised God for his mouth kissing and suckling my folds with his lips, for his gentle thumb circling my clitoris as his tongue slowly probed my pussy.

I grabbed the back of his head to keep from fainting and falling, forcing his tongue deeper into me, sending currents through my entire body. When he slid his hands to my nipple, I couldn't keep myself upright and buckled.

He caught me as I fell, and twisted my body slowly to the floor, his mouth still drinking from my well, one hand beneath my head, the other beneath my ass.

Then, as if it were some dance ritual, Thomas cradled me like a babe to his chest, lifting me up in a dizzying whirl as his cock found its new home inside me.

He raised himself to his knees, lifting me along the length of his torso, as if I were his marionette.

And when I could no longer hold back, I wrapped my arms around his neck, gripping him as I spun my hips to match his deliberate rhythm, his choreography, his cadence – and then, at last, as his breath quickened in time with mine, he moaned and shuddered.

And I felt him explode, a piercing hot stream. As for my own release, the feel of his seed was a summons calling forth my own flood, which gathered mass and heat as the `tides began to swell.`

`As if by gravity and pressure, my pussy collapsed upon itself, a wet star going supernova, as the waves crashed around us in the surf.`

*

Meghan closes the folder and looks out the window.

A stream of white puffs the glass and disintegrates. Melts. The clear blue of day and sky and sex shines iridescent light and fades into a gray. "Now I'm wet and can't concentrate—here, feel this."

She halfway smiles and unzips her pants for my hand to dip into. And she leads me into the elastic shield of lace and cotton, under which I feel tufts of coarse hair trailing down to slippery skin, warm and moist.

Her pelvis jolts upward into my fingers lightly fumbling between her folds, caressing and savoring the touch. My cock jumps when she takes my finger and slides it into her.

Her lips are slick like oil, like sweat, like saliva.

My finger moves in and out of her. She thrusts upward softly, cooing like a shuddering bird. My finger like a little cock, I move slow, easy, slow, slide, easy. She moans as I find the nub of her clit and make circles. Then, with two fingers, I slide into her ever-so-warm-and-wet—*my sweet lord.*

"Baby," she whispers, her hips grinding as we find a rhythm, "faster, there. Just a little bit faster. There, there, right there. Christ, don't you stop. Don't...."

I smell musk now, just a hint of it. Like the mountain soil, rich with the smells of earth and woman.

Meghan is both.

She shifts as I lift my fingers and probe quietly and intensely deeper. I feel her shudder building. She moans and stiffens, bites her bottom lip as my thumb rubs along her clit in several long, slow circles. I can tell she's close. Her eyes close to a mid-shut. Her focus lingers about three inches in front of her flushed face. Her breaths come in short bursts.

Her ass lifts from the seat as she arcs her back and—

I nearly swerve us off the mountain when she comes.

I try not to watch her easing off her pleasure high. I try to drive carefully and safely. But it's no easy feat, that. From my periphery, I note the changes from orgasm to post-bliss. I am laughing now. "God, I love it when you come. Your face turns me on."

"What was that?" she asks, exasperated. "The hell with Gary's rule. How can we get through this folder without having some kind of release, you know?"

"Hey, we didn't break his rule—he said no FUCKING," I tell her. "We didn't fuck, I assure you. And I should know because I've had a hard-on for almost twelve hours."

Meghan slaps my arm.

And we sit in comfortable silence until she orders me to pull the car over so she can give me head. Unfortunately, I have a problem.

"I have to pee."

"I said pull over," Meghan whispers, still in a post-orgasmic glow. "Overlook area up ahead. You can go by the picnic tables. Besides, I'm hungry. We can eat too. I packed a few protein bars and you still have the soda."

"I'm hungry and horny."

"And you have to urinate, poor baby. Hope you can pee with that stiffy—wait, it can't be that bad, can it? Oh, my. I was wrong—this needs some medicine."

"Yes, it does," I say, matter-of-fact as I pull to an overlook.

Car engine off. I adjust my pants. We get out and stroll toward the picnic area. And she's acting all innocent-like, with her blue-gray eyes staring through me, looking down my throat, my stomach, down through my intestines, bladder, urethra, and then out the head of my swollen cock.

Meghan leads me to the worn table, her hands on my pants, my zipper and button coming apart in her fingers, my boxers down to my ankles, my bouncing red cock set free. The need to urinate is almost as bad as my need to ejaculate.

And what does Meghan do?

She talks directly to my penis, grabbing the shaft and tapping it like a microphone.

"Is this thing on," she says, kissing and running her tongue on and around the tip. "Don't be so hard on my boyfriend, Mr. Penis," she says, slipping the tip into her mouth and then slowing pulling it out. "He's got to pee, Mr. Penis, so please let him pee. Please, let him pee for me."

Then she looks up at me with a baby doe-eyed smile, with my wet dick bouncing in the cold mountain wind. And I swear to fucking Christ, I'm going to lose my fucking mind.

My erection subsides long enough for me to make some fucking water. As urine slowly and then sharply streams from my prick, Meghan kisses the shaft. "I want to drink it—would that turn you on? If I tasted it? Would it be too dirty if I put you in my mouth and swallowed your piss like cum?"

With a jerk, I sit up.

For a moment—and it's only for a moment, I nearly tell her to do it. My cock is still hard, and it does sound naughty and filthy.

Instead, I just watch her kiss me until I'm done urinating.

She flicks my cock, squeezing it at the base to make sure I don't lose my erection, until the clear liquid drips cease.

Finally, I say, "How incredible it would be if we could have sex on this mountain, right here and now in broad daylight, with nothing but God and passing cars to catch glimpses of my pumping ass."

Meghan giggles.

"I don't want to be arrested," she says with a naughty grin. "But there are other options."

My cock still in her hand, she leads over to the left side of the table, the part hidden beneath a tree, and urges me to lie down. Shielded from passing cars as I now am, she slides the tormenting thing, my accursed swollen splinter, inside her mouth.

And Meghan, God bless her, begins to heal my tortured prominence.

Above me, the mist and sun, the clouds and mountain air—below me, her warm tongue and lips.

As dutiful as a very dedicated, sexually gifted Florence Nightingale, my woman draws out the venom from my snakebite, slowly and with care. I buckle on the table and gasp, pumping her face as she sucks the hot white poison into her mouth, swallowing each diminishing explosion.

Meghan releases me and restores my shrinking manhood into its sheath, zipping me up and pulling me to my feet. "We should go," she says. "Maybe we should run."

"Why hurry?"

From the trail below us, I hear wolf-whistles and hearty applause. Beneath a huge maple tree to our direct right is another picnic table, barely visible, and two hollering hikers—where did they come from? I shake my head in dismay.

Embarrassment?

A little.

Excitement mixed with a perverted sense of pride? More than I expect.

Meghan laughs, waves an acknowledgment to the couple, and wipes her mouth in a big theatrical swoop with the back of her hand. She gets in the car while I lay there like a rock on the table, the sounds of distant laughing echoing around me now.

"Let's go, lover," she calls to me. "Hurry up, baby!"

And so, I get to my feet, pull up my pants, and bow to our audience.

*

Truth Unhinged

> *For you, I shall be the wolf. I shall run on all fours. I shall hunt for you, taste blood for you. I wish to fill the hole in your heart, where time echoes and hope ferries pain from chamber to vein, and you search for my song finding only ever your lonely voice. O, but I am there, mistress. I am trapped, broken, and buried, but I am there. It seems we must be separated, as night and dawn. If this is to be, then l gladly lie in wait for your rise and howl as you wax and wane until the sun rises and we begin the dance again.*
>
> —Simone Simon, from *Precipice*

RAIN LIGHTLY PELTS THE WINDSHIELD. Fog undulates across the highway and up stony edifices to our left. We enter mountain tunnels burrowed by mechanical moles some years ago. Cars in front are driving too slow to pass. The radio is a soft murmur of piano keys and violin strings, the sound of melancholy, of blue moodiness, of bittersweet partings.

"Do you think most people are reduced to animals?" Meghan suddenly asks.

"Reduced to what? Animals?"

"Yes, because I was unhinged back there. I almost drank your piss—thank God, I didn't, but it was so deliciously, delightfully naughty to think about doing. Oh, I was close to doing it. That thought of being so filthy with you became a driving need. Touching the taboo—GOD, it's fucking hot to tickle the devil's ass. You can't tell me that there's not a part of you that wouldn't love to just give yourself over to every single sick, twisted, demented fantasy. Oh, I want to fuck you in front of a bunch of people. Promise me you'll think about fucking me in front of a bunch of people."

"Like that woman and her husband?"

"No, that's just exhibitionism, which I love," she says. "I was thinking of something naughtier, something we haven't done together before. And don't tell me you weren't thinking about it. I know what you like. I know what turns you on, baby."

Of course, she's right.

"I think Carol and Gary have ulterior motives," I tell her. "They might be exactly who they say they are. They may want to help us too, but I can tell they got 'scheme' jizzed all over their faces."

The rain has stopped.

The fog is thick like sea foam and gray polyfill.

"So, what do you think?" I ask.

Meghan laughs. "I don't know and honestly don't know—I've

been thinking about watching you fuck Gary in the ass while he fucks Carol as goes down on me. I can't get that out of my head."

I burst out laughing. "Is that in our folder too?"

The fog lifts momentarily. We can see the road now. The sky is not so gray, and the clouds have descended in patches across the Parkway. In the sky, a swath of blue marking daylight and time. The sun is nowhere, everywhere, and the view is too beautiful to watch in a cramped little car seat.

Meghan reads my mind. "Pull over—we need to see this. There's an overlook up ahead. See?"

I do see.

I pull over and park. "Jesus Christ, what a view."

We get out and walk to the railing. The stony clearing behind it teeters on a steep cliff of evergreen and rock. Meghan holds my hand and gasps. Around us, Appalachian beauty from every angle. Our hearts are oohing and ahhing at the vastness of it, the grandeur and majesty of it.

We are wrapped in awe.

There are two things in the world that humble me:

One is sitting on a beach at night, the moon shining iridescence above an ocean whose crashing clockwork of waves keeps time below.

And the other is standing on the edge of a mountain.

The sheer joy and exhilarating thrill of being there, tucked under the low ceiling of clouds. I go into a strange psychedelic euphoria not unlike the rise before a really good orgasm. I am kinetically linked to mountains. They are sexually dangerous, predatory and erotically invincible—to stand in this place arouses me.

I feel like fucking Zeus.

Meghan sighs. "This is breathtaking."

"Yes, it is," I tell her, pulling her body into mine. "I'd jump if it meant fucking you first."

She giggles. "My, Grandma, what a great big cock you have."

It's my turn to laugh.

I want to crawl so deep inside this moment that I'll be lost to time for always.

Oh, how the earth breathes in those spaces between the tick and the tock. Humility comes when you face such greatness. And it is in those quiet moments, when you are a spec on the pendulum of All Things, when you are suddenly aware that you are also swinging with the tide and the mountains, that you are in sync with their motion, that they are sharing in your journey through the cosmos.

The smells of nature are rejuvenating. The sap of trees, the green slick of their leaves, the soil holding their trunks and roots, the mountain beneath all of it. For a moment, I get dizzy and nearly stumble backward. Meghan squeezes my hand and steadies me.

We turn back to the view. She starts to hum, and then she sings a little melody. It echoes like a waterfall, a hush-hushing lulling sound, like the melodic breath of a Celtic faerie. Her voice is so lovely I want to cry. It's been ages since I last heard her sing. She never sings in public (not like this attention-grabbing karaoke whore). My pulse races as her voices spills over the edge of the mountain and into the unseen valley beneath us.

Yes, I want to crawl inside this one moment.

"We should go," she says, abruptly ending her song.

And I sigh.

Meghan often rape her own beauty.

A quick turn of the head, tears on her cheeks. She tries to smile as she wipes her cheek. "I got a chill for some reason," she says. "I don't know why I'm so sad."

Back in the car, the silence is heavy with too much stillness, too much reflection.

There is fear on her face and an occasional tear. Her head, normally so poised, looks almost cartoonish as it wobbles and bobbles. She wipes another tear and blinks.

"Are we crazy?"

A loaded question, that is.

"Maybe," I reply honestly, "but still together aren't we?"

She sighs.

More silence.

"Do you want to hit the folder again?" I ask her. "It might help."

Meghan shakes her head. "Did it ever cross your mind that maybe I fucked those men because YOU fucked ME up?" she asks. "Maybe you've been the worst thing that EVER happened to me."

I slam on the brakes and swerve to the shoulder.

Meghan swallows a lump and wipes her face with her sleeve. "I knew this was a gamble—I knew it, I knew it, I knew it," she whispers, shaking her head. "It was too sudden, taking this fucking trip together. We have way too much history that's ugly and painful."

"What's wrong, Meghan?"

"I don't FUCKING KNOW!" she screams. "If you aren't questioning why we're doing this, Joss, then you're still the same fool you always were."

"You can't run forever, Meghan. I love you."

"I know, and it pisses me off, Joss," she says. "God damn you, I'm beyond broken from your love. Deep down, I hate you for it. I can't let that feeling go, and I can't move on. You can pretend all you want that we're going to be okay, but I can't."

"Why MUST you keep punishing me?"

"Because you don't punish me," she says. "You know it turns me on, and I want you to punish me, and I don't want you to punish me. I'm a fucking hot mess, and I want to not feel like I am."

A car passes by, honks its horn, and disappears.

We sit in silence.

"What's gotten into you? What's wrong?"

Meghan doesn't answer.

Her face brightens with the thought of something to say, but then it fades back to a forbidden zone again. A wasteland of symphonic silence I can only try to sense with fuzzy probing.

What the fuck—*whatthefuckwhatthefuckwhatthefuck?*

"Meghan."

"Joss, am I worth it to you, what we're doing?"

"Is it worth it to you?"

She shrugs. I can tell she's not telling me something, and something important. She tends to pout when she's lost in one of her struggles against herself. "Maybe we should just fuck our brains out tonight and then try to move on with our lives when we get back to Atlanta. I'm not good for you. You're not good for me—why are we doing this to each other?"

"Quit fucking saying that!"

A longer silence.

Meghan sniffs. "Don't yell at me."

"Goddammit, why not? I have a right to be angry!"

"I never told you to stop being angry," she counters, "just don't yell at me in the car. It's too loud and my head hurts. I knew this was going to happen."

"And you know the reason why," I spit back. "Would you like me to unpack one of the wine bottles for you to chug while we fight? God knows you can't be sober longer than three hours, Meghan. It might be time for your medicine—you know, to take the edge off."

I turn off the engine.

Another turtle-paced car honks and passes us, wending its way around the side of the mountain and out of sight. Meghan sniffs. "I don't want to fight anymore. Let's just get to Cherokee and have one more nice night," she says, sinking back into her seat. "Or you could just slip your finger inside me again and ease this tension."

The fog is rolling in thick around us. I can barely see the view from the road now. Taking a deep breath, I start the car and continue our drive. After what feels forever, I take her hand. "Please, don't shut me out."

Meghan snorts, looking out her window, staring at the gray distance, her breath fogging the glass. "I want a bed and you naked beside me. And pot—I really want to get baked and fuck my brains out. That's what I want."

"It isn't a bad idea," I tell her.

"What about with Carol and Gary? That a bad idea?"

I can't answer her, because I honestly don't know.

*

I remember reading a letter to Penthouse about this guy and his wife. They were happily married, loved each other. He and his neighbor were talking and they wanted to both do the guy's wife at the same time, right? A little relationship-spicy-spruce-thing.

The wife was into doing both guys. They got together one night and fucked. Well, the husband was also a fireman, and he had to go do his fire thing. They were right in the middle of their naughty threesome when he gets a call.

So, he leaves, assuming his buddy and wifey will stop until he gets back from the call. A couple of hours later, hubby comes home to find buddy and wifey still fucking. A hanging-from-the-rafters kind of fucking all by themselves. They took advantage of the moment and assumed that if the hubby OK'd them fucking with him then they could do it without him too.

Then there was what happened in Oneida, New York, mid-1800s.

The same company that makes silverware, flatware, and cutlery sprung from the ashes of the first utopia based on free love. Free love in the eyes of God, at any rate, and it worked for many years.

They found that restricting partners, confining them to only one person, was ridiculous. And blasphemous. It detracted from the purpose of exalting the Creator. Their philosophy was that we should love all others, that THAT was true love, THAT was true humanity.

By maintaining others in a secluded household was considered selfish and, in the Eyes of God, unholy. A man named Noyes founded the place with his wife. Eventually, the monogamists that inevitably sprouted within the community were too much of a strong faction by the time of its downfall. The communal marriage ended after thirty years. His son, ironically, was a little usurper. Anyway, my point is this: they found sex with multiple people to be liberating, joyous, ceremonious, a blessing heaven would bestow.

For a time, it was a success, so I contemplate the proposition that it's not all bad. It has been a great, if slightly fucked-up, week though. Still, this trip might solve some of the problems we're too afraid to name.

Why do I get the feeling I'm being groomed for something?

And why do I get the feeling Meghan is behind it?

"The thought of fucking Gary and Carol turns me on," she says. "It turns you on too. Don't deny it. I won't deny it. I can tell you're excited about the thought." Her hand is in my lap. "THIS never lies, baby."

She's right. I am on fire.

"Do you like that, me rubbing you while you think about me with someone else, you watching me watching you with someone else," she says, "you taking Gary's cock in your ass, me taking it in mine, and then my mouth."

Lust rising and falling.

Jealousy filling and draining. Heart pounding and brain assaulted with images. Knuckles white from the heat of my hands gripping the steering wheel.

And I am on fire.

"Let's get back to the folder," I say. "Any stories?"

Meghan looks through the pages. "No, just a transcript and a CD track."

*

Carol's Voice:

"So, tell me why you love the rain."

Woman's Voice:

"Because my husband doesn't. Because I met someone else who does. I met him online. We email and IM each other when I can sneak away from bed. I meet him for dinner when my husband goes out of town. I see the man more because of the rain."

Carol's Voice:

"Explain what you mean by that. And let yourself go, Judy, exactly as we discussed in your session. Close your eyes and speak freely. Speak to me as if you were the author of your own erotic story. Speak to me as if I were the husband you've wanted Frank to be. Speak to me as if your husband and the man you had the affair with are one and the same. He'll love you for telling the truth."

Woman's Voice:

"And you want me to use the words we talked about?"

Carol's Voice:

"Yes, none of them is an evil, honey. Take your time and start when you're ready. Okay?"

*

We have dinner one evening, an early dinner, my secret lover and me. He tells me that it's going to rain as we walk back to the parking garage. And he's right. As soon as we get to the stairwell, the skies open, and the rain comes down in buckets.

So, we're in the stairwell, kissing as we sit on the bottom step. It's hot inside, so we crack the door. The wind blows it shut. Our kissing becomes something else entirely. His hands are like fire on my body, electricity, lightning. The stairwell is half-lit with a flickering overhead light that buzzes like an exposed wire.

Outside you can hear the rain and the thunder. We're in this semi-dark place, staring at each other, kissing each other. He pulls me closer to him. And I want him right there, this man of heat and bad weather. His face is shadow and sweat, and it makes me become this other thing, this animal. I want to taste his skin, to lick it and taste it. I'm scared and excited, and I'm beading with my own sweat.

Thunder shakes the garage.

This man who isn't my husband moves his lips over my mouth. I taste salt and water and heat, smell the wine on his breath. When I hear his voice, deep and low just inside the tunnel of my ear, my heart begins to pound, and the moisture between my legs begins to flow. I am thunder and rain. Because of the heat and his voice, I am melting now. I groan when I hear it. I can't tell you what his voice does to me.

It's like something from a dream and he knows me.

And I want him to know my body. I need him to know it. This yearning is making me go into spasms, and I can't breathe. I only crave. I must have him now, as the rain pours and thunder shakes, I must have him. I feel his mouth on my neck, his hands on my waist, his body against mine as he drinks of my sweat, his tongue thrilling my flesh.

And his tongue darts across my throat, my face, and my ears.

I shudder. I feel like fainting. I am hungry and dazed, ravenous and wild. He licks between my breasts. I feel his hands on my thighs, caressing and teasing, coming closer to that place, my center, my – it's shaking. I'm shaking. My-my-my – my pussy – it, I mean, SHE quivers. I mean, I am quivering. And I never quiver. I don't let myself go enough to just quiver like that. But I swear to God, I am quivering, from – oh, what did I read the other day?

Ah, from tits to taint!

Can you believe this? I don't. I barely know this man and he has me quivering. From his gaze, his kissing, his heat, his hands touching me. Christ, I can't take it. I reach for him – feel his hardness. But I don't dare give in. I want it to last. I want to keep feeling his tongue over me. I feel his hands at the button of my shorts; he rips them open and pulls them off, tears them from me. He's on his knees now and he stares at my soaked panties and moans as he buries his head there, breathing me, tasting me.

The sky thunders and shakes the garage.

I run my fingers through his now sweating hair and I lean down to smell it as he rests his face and mouth near my clit. He smells warm and sweet. I feel his breath on me – and then he rips my clothes away. I am on fire, and I just burst – a loud scream. Sharp, quick – I come so fast. But it's so small – so small when I know what ELSE is coming – what I feel, it rises again. I moan as his mouth creeps closer to my lips. I know he wants to drink more of me, I feel his desire, his need. And I know I am gushing in his face – and I imagine me as this goddess fountain and he's bathing in my waters.

My shirt, my six hundred dollar blouse my husband bought for my birthday, he rips it off, and I am shuddering and shaking all the more for it. I am drenched in sweat and heat and orgasm. My nipples are sensitive – the air hurts them, teases them – and I feel moisture just pouring, pouring from between me, like I'm bleeding water, like down my thighs, I am just gushing from desire. I am raining, in my pussy, I am raining.

For him, for this man.

I don't know when he removes his – he – how did he-- when did he – he's just suddenly naked – I see his cock standing and I – I just – buckle. I drop. I have no control – I am out of my mind. I am so much no more a – but I have never felt more like – I am this cat woman, I swear to God. And I want his semen in me – on me – all over my face, my neck, my breasts, my pussy – all over of me like some whore.

And his hard prick – God. I want to taste it, to feel it in my mouth, to tease it and suck it. I – he can't hold me back – I just – I take it in and swallow it down to the back of my throat – my lips touch its base and feel the nest of hair. I can taste him, his drops of cum in my throat. Just drops.

He moans and thrusts. I begin moving my mouth up and down his shaft, licking him, feeling his manhood. I'm milking him, slow and easy, as his cock glides into and out of me. With a hand, I fondle his balls, lifting and lightly tugging at them as my other hands – well, I'm fingering myself, playing with my clit.

I am not me, not my body – I am lightning. I am thunder. He pulls his cock from my mouth. He helps me stand. My hands find his shoulders, and I push him down. It's time I make him summon my thunder again. He goes down on me without hesitation or complaint – ah, what a gift he is – and before I can blink I feel his tongue between my lips. He tongue flicks my clit and drinks me. Slowly, he swallows as I melt into his mouth.

Lightning crashes, and my thunder answers again and again. I grip the railing when he puts his arms around me to support me as he eats me. He won't stop eating me, devouring me, draining my fluids. I beg for him to stop – he won't stop. He won't stop. Then, as if in slow motion, he rises and buries his cock inside me. Slow. So, so, slow, so unbearably slow. I scream in agony, and I know he's ready to explode so I pull him from my pussy and guide him into my ass.

I want the pain and the pleasure to mingle there. And his cock is so slick from my pussy juices that it glides in easy. His body jerks, he rears his head back, and he cries – the light flickers as his body goes rigid and he explodes in my ass. His semen spills down my legs in great streams that don't stop. I pull him out of my ass and offer him my pussy, which he pumps, and his cum doesn't stop.

It doesn't stop.

And he's still moaning and pumping, and he's still coming.

A lightning flash before the echoing thunder, a gush of wind opens the door and closes it. You can hear the trees just outside blowing in the sideways rain. I feel his breath on my cooling back. He is inside me, beside me now, behind me on the stairs, pulling me to him, kissing me fiercely. Holding me so tightly, so much like the man I needed my husband to be. The flickering light dies in the stairwell, and then we're in blackness. And like thunder he whispers low into my ear how much he loves the rain.

*

Another silence after Meghan finishes reading. It's raining now, a light drizzle.

I fucking hate the rain.

I think about moments in my life when rain affected it or me, my experiences of both or either. It seems to rain whenever I am facing some monumental decision or formative happenstance that has yet to reveal itself. It's not God-fearing, fire and brimstone rain—it's the childlike rain that puts you to sleep, the misty rain that covers you in a vaporous sheen. The unassuming rain is the water of seduction, of dark temptation, of treachery and deceit, and apparently, as it was for that parking garage woman, the depraved animal need for sweaty hot anal sex.

Don't you love the rain?

No, I hate the rain.

I move back in time to think about the weekend I left Meghan. I try to remember the details about the day and the reasons. Why did I leave her? What happened and in what order? What was said and done, what was left unsaid and undone?

Much was left, before and since.

I can't help but wonder where we are really going, what we are really doing. I drive through the rain, and I smile because I'm imagining she's going to tell me she's a lesbian now and wants to share her partner with me. That her partner is waiting for us at the hotel in Cherokee. That her partner happens to be Carol and Gary's daughter. It's something I'd never thought about before, but now that it's raining and I'm thinking to myself, I'm curious as to how that arrangement might work.

I imagine it oh so clearly.

Voluptuous Meghan's long dark hair and olive skin contrasts her new lover's green eyes and perfect milky flesh, her short red hair and tight pixie body.

Don't you love the rain?

No, I don't—I hate the rain.

And then I think of Ben, sweet angelic Ben, brilliant and talented, small and passionate. How he loved me and how I didn't love him. And oh, how I wanted to love him. I grip the steering wheel harder. I want to punish Meghan for touching Ben, for finding him and telling him lies, for putting her poisons all over that sweet man's heart. I still remember my week with him.

For six days, it rained. And then we said goodbye.

My mind starts to drift toward Carol and Gary Rider, these angelic, holistically open, and magical people. Were they too good to be true?

"Joss?"

I don't answer.

"Joss?"

"Hmm? Oh, Meghan, I'm sorry."

"Where are you, sweetheart?"

"I was thinking about Gary and Carol and wondering what they're really about," I tell her.

Which is partly true.

"Wondering what they're about? What do you think that is?"

"I don't know—they just seem too good to be true," I admit with a sigh. "Look, we can talk about it after I stop for gas at that station up there. Want something sweet?"

Meghan shrugs. "Nah, club soda's fine," she says, taking my hand. Pulling next to the pump, I head to the cashier, who directs me to the refrigerator in back with the sodas. For the life of me, I can't shake this whole therapy trip—it just feels like so much of the timing was perfect. We happened to be at the right place at the right time, met the right people who happen to be wealthy and crunchy granola folk who want nothing more than to help strangers heal.

I buy the club soda for Meghan, a candy bar for me, and I pre-pay for the gas. As I turn to leave, I spy a row of faces taped to the glass door. The faces of eight missing young men and women, all of them close to my age.

"What's happened to them?" I ask the man behind the counter.

He wipes his nose with his sleeve. "Started happening 'bout a year ago," he says. "Young couples from Chattanooga, Dahlonega, Cherokee, and two hikers from Tennessee. Those are just the ones who've been through here a time or two."

"Serial killer?" I ask.

The attendant shrugs. "No bodies have turned up," he says. "Me personally, I think it has more to do with that cult down there in northern Georgia, some military-type compound west of Cherokee. I hear rumors about that place all the time, most of 'em untrue I'd wager, but a few seem to have more truth when you think about those faces there."

"What are the rumors?"

"Weird shit, sexual deviant shit," he replies, eyes darting around to check for bystanders and their uninvited ears. "You want the tame stuff or the shithouse crazy stuff?"

*

Preflight

> *Augustin, lie down on the bed. Eugenie, you recline in his arms while I sodomize you, I'll frig your clitoris with the head of Augustin's superb prick. And Augustin will take good care not to discharge. Gentle Chevalier will have the kindness to arrange himself upon Eugenie's shoulders so as to expose his fine buttocks to my kisses. I'll frig him again, and so shall I have my engine in an ass and a prick in each hand. And you, Madame, after having been your master, I want you to become mine. Buckle on the most gigantic of your dildos. Fit it about your loins and spare me not!*
>
> *—Marquis de Sade, from Philosophy in the Bedroom*

THE ATTENDANT APOLOGIZES FOR THE GRAPHIC DETAILS, which are as plentiful as are the number of separate rumors. He seems to think half of them are closer to the truth than not. He apologizes again, and I tell him not to worry. "I asked for the crazy," I remind him. "You gave me crazy."

"I know, but it's—I don't know," he says.

With a nod of thanks, I head back to the car, fill it up, and get us back to the road with a strange weight on my shoulders. We're on the last leg of the trip before we stop for the night, and I open my already sexually assaulted brain to more crazy.

And it's so beyond reality, I just let go of those rumors.

Still, as Meghan sips her soda, I don't touch my candy bar. All I see are the faces of those people, young faces of men and women our age—something odd kept tickling the back of my brain about the rumors regarding them.

"Joss?"

"What? Where what?"

"Your mind—where is it?"

"I don't know," I tell her. "I'm tired. It's been a long day. I'm beyond horny. We're losing light and we've got a way left to go."

Then we hit a fog bank. Brake lights of a snaking row of cars ahead. Now we're driving at a crawl. Shit, I can't avoid this anymore.

"Meghan, when you were booking hotels for this trip, did you book Carol and Gary Rider? I'm not accusing you—I'm just trying to set things upright in my head."

"You won't get mad if I say yes?"

I laugh. "No, I won't—I'll be relieved."

Meghan takes my hand. "Then yes, I did," she says with a sigh. "I was HOPING you'd ask me. They had a few ads on Craigslist, so I looked them up. They're real, Joss. Licensed couples counselors and sex therapists, the ranch, the BLUE erotic stuff, the number of clients over the years. As soon as I spoke to them, I knew they'd help us. I just didn't want you to be angry with me for not telling you."

"Why would I be angry at you?"

She wipes her face. "I need help too—not just because of us."

"I know."

"I want to remake our pain into something else, Joss."

"I do too."

"I want to remake my sins."

"I do too."

"I want to forgive myself and you for everything that happened," Meghan says, taking my hand, her breath shuddering. "And I want to forgive myself and you for what hasn't happened yet. I want to be okay with wanting the things I want, with you wanting the things you want—it's not like those desires define us."

"No, they don't."

She sniffs, takes a sip from her soda. "How are we going to do this?"

Shaking my head, I laugh and shrug. "I don't know—we might not need to do anything but talk to each other, listen to each other."

She giggles. "Write naughty stories for each other," she says. "Perform them for other people. Help contribute to BLUE.

"Exactly, yes, and then after we do, we call it a day and go back to Atlanta."

The silence that follows is comfortable, or so I tell myself. The cars are moving again. And we are facing the next part of our trip more unified than ever before.

Meghan giggles. "Why are we so preoccupied with size? Women's breasts, men's dicks, women's asses, men's balls? I don't know why I was thinking about it—just popped in my head. Are you preoccupied with size? I think my breasts are too small. I hate them."

"Speak for yourself—I love your breasts," I say. "I always picture yours whenever I have titty-fucking fantasies."

"Shut-up, asshole—I'm being serious."

"So, do you imagine a giant fantasy cock or one like mine?"

"Yours is beyond fantasy, thank you very much," she says, adding, "as I have seen and felt more than my fair share of dicks. You have no idea how gifted you are."

"Liar," I tell her.

She slaps my arm. "Shut up, I am not," she says, "and let me tell you this: what you got in your pants would scare the shit out of half the women I know. But every once in a while, I do entertain something unreal—and I mean circus elephant unreal, horse unreal. If I'm feeling like a—well, if I'm in that frame of mind is all."

"Honey, it's okay—just tell me."

"You are the one in 9 out of 10 of my fantasies, Joss."

"Even with women?"

Meghan smiles. "Uh, no dick is near my mind when I'm with a woman," she says. "But if I fantasize about women, I tend to imagine big bouncy tits—like Carol has."

I laugh.

After a thoughtful silence, I say, “Do you trust Carol and Gary?”

Meghan nods. “Well, I think they’ll help us find the answers,” she says, looking out the window. “Why do I crave so much attention from other men? Why do I despise you for your split desires when mine are fractured into shards? Why must I be at the center of all men’s lusts and desires? Why do I get turned on by hurting you with it? Why do you accept that in me while I refuse to extend the same courtesy to you?”

“It’s why I didn’t come back, Meghan.”

“Then why’d you leave?”

Another long silence.

I think of this woman with whom I am struggling to find truth. A balance. A place we can explore together, side by side, following our rules. I smile.

And then she smiles.

I don’t answer her question, and she knows it.

“I can’t believe we’re talking and not screaming,” Meghan says. “Carol and Gary are miracle workers for helping us get to this place alone. I’m glad we made this trip.” Her sudden sigh fogs her window. “I wonder why I feel so insecure.”

“About us?”

Blue eyes pierce me with a hard stare and fat tears down her face. “Being without you these past two years has been the worst time of my life. And now, I don’t think I have ever been more in love with you."

"Then why are you crying?"

She looks out the window, misty dappled sun shadows across her smooth face. She's swallowing and thinking. Her bottom lip quivers. She shakes her head, wipes her eyes, refuses to speak the words that might weaken her. We drive in silence, keeping thoughts private. I think of those last months we were together. And then the last weekend, the day after I watched her with Ben.

Why Ben?

If she had fucked any other man, I would've stayed.

So, my fist met the window in the bedroom, cutting up my hand and wrists. Of all things to punch—the sheet rock on the wall, the wooden door, the pillows, the side of the washing machine—I broke a window like an idiot, leaving the mess for her to clean. I glance at the knuckles on my hand, the faded scars there. It's hard to forget that night, harder still to forgive myself for what I did. To Meghan, and even to Ben.

I never should've bought those self-portraits she painted with him.

"Joss, what's wrong?"

I look at my hand and flex my fingers. "I was thinking we might have a chance," I tell her, hoping it isn't a lie. "And I'm wondering about Carol and Gary's intentions."

Meghan ignores that last comment. "What's that sign say?"

"Cherokee Village in twenty minutes," I reply. "Where are we staying tonight?"

"The only Best Western in North Georgia," Meghan says with a giggle. "Carol and Gary want us to join them for dinner and drinks when we get settled. They said they have something special planned."

"I want a long hot shower with your naked body next to mine first," I tell her.

Meghan takes my hand and squeezes it in lockstep time with the swish-swish of the windshield wipers.

"Is there anything left in the folder to read?" I ask.

"There's one story—a note from Carol says she picked it for me to read to you."

I snort. "Whatever that means."

Meghan giggles. "Right? Ooh, I like the way this one begins," she says, settling back into her seat. "Amber is such a beautiful name. Early in the summer, I met a stripper named Amber—well, she used to be a stripper. Anyway, I'm getting all tingly again."

I shake my head. "So, read already."

Meghan clears her throat. "It's written by a woman named Simone for BLUE Magazine and called, 'One Pair, Two of a Kind.'"

*

Amber sat on a weathered park bench one cloudy afternoon smoking her cigarette. Camels. No filter. Bitch with brass balls. Wrapped in the blanket of private thoughts, oblivious to the presence of the mysterious man watching her.

Amber fixed her eyes on the last butt she had expectorated a moment ago. Chain smoking. Great habit. Cancerous habit. Gunk the lungs with all kinds of goodies. Fuck it. Loneliness does that to a girl. Makes her smoke. Inhaling and exhaling, carbon monoxide from hell.

She finished her second stick.

"Just like a penis. Screws you just like one." Look up into the hazy sky. Light another. Smile.

Amber felt another presence somewhere around her space. Peripherally, she sensed him. Her personal space extended many meters about her. Accustomed to the detached area in which she interacted and observed and lived. But detached. From trusting. From health. From life. Personal space, but nothing is personal any more. People give each other blow jobs in alleyways, fuck on park benches, mug you, rape you.

Personal space, my ass.

An invisible force field quasi-protecting her and warning her. That's it. Personal space as smoke detector. Field alerts her to anyone who breaches it. Usually, she even senses the type of person who invades. Tremendous barrier she's adopted since Kevin.

"Asshole," she muttered to herself.

A shadow moved from behind the wide oak tree that hung like knobby arthritic spiders overhead. The shadow had a voice.

"May I sit, or was that comment for me?"

Amber shuddered. The shadow was, what,

British? Irish? She loved accents, especially thick brogues. This man, dark complexion, gypsy-like, this man that now occupied the empty seat next to her, was the kind of man she only saw on television.

"I've been watching you," he confessed as he removed his long wool coat.

"I know," Amber stated, shuddering, frightened a bit, glancing at a nearby picnic table. Huddled birds fighting for food scraps. Pigeons. Related to the dove, ironic. You can eat dove. Pigeons are full of worms. Flying rats, a friend of hers from London told her. "For about how long?"

Kevin's a flying rat.

"Well, a few moments behind the tree, but about an hour from over there." He pointed to the gazebo that marked the entrance to the park. A small family had gathered inside now. The man draped the coat across his lap.

"Why in hell would you watch me for that long? All I was doing was--"

"Smoking, yes, I know. Peculiar habit, but then again, so am I."

Amber noticed he had bright green eyes.

He continued to speak. "I have been wondering, Miss, who broke your heart."

Amber was aghast. "How did you – what do you want? Who are you?"

"A purveyor, Miss – I'd say pervert, but I don't want to frighten you."

"Fuck off, you Limey Bastard – I'm not afraid of a pervert," Amber said, with a snort of disbelief. "My uncle was a pervert his whole life and told the funniest fucking stories. Sit."

The stranger blushed. "Thank you, Miss — I am a sexual deviant."

Amber looked at him thoughtfully and shrugged. "Me too, Professor Perv — wait, you're not going to cut me up and fuck my bloody pieces, are you?"

The man laughs. "So cheeky — I like that, I do like that so much."

"Why me? I'm nobody. A cheeky nobody."

"My dear, you most certainly are somebody," he said with a side-glancing grin. "Now, I will have you know that I followed you from the Italian restaurant and watched you sitting here from behind that tree. Speechlessness doesn't become you, Amber. You were quite a chatterbox to that dashing young man who sauntered by a few moments ago. I'm assuming you prefer the muscular type — your eyes never left his round backside as he strolled off toward the city. I bet you prefer your muscular men to be hairier than your leaner male specimens, yes? Unless they're short, of course — in that case, you want shorn all over, from coin purse to taint to asshole."

"Jesus Christ, how do you know all this?"

The man leaned over to Amber and thrust a finger next to his eye. "I am an excellent judge of character and a keen observer, Miss Amber Somebody. I must say I've had quite the erection being near you today."

"Fucking hell," Amber said as she grabbed her purse and made to leave. "I don't talk to creeps unless I'm getting paid to do it. Have a nice day."

"Please," the man pleaded. "I swear I won't harm you, Miss Amber Somebody."

"How do you know my name?"

The man shrugged. "Like I said, I'm a good listener."

Intrigued by his mystery and dark handsome face, Amber slowly put her purse on the ground next to her feet and said, "What would you like to talk about?"

The man lifted his coat a little, just wide enough for Amber to see the erection he still sported. His short penis curved in an upward arc – the tip of it glistened with a bead of semen, the shaft pulsed. Amber continued to stare at it as she lit another cigarette, moving her head to the side to see it from a different angle too. She smiled and waved her hand. "Impressive," she said. "Put it away for now."

The man nodded and chuckled as he closed the flap and buried a hand in the pocket above his erection. He let out a long sigh. "Tell me about this boy you loved."

Amber exhaled. "I tend to mix my verb tenses when I tell stories, so... Kevin was a dog, but I loved him the moment I first saw him in his Goodwill jeans, flannel shirt, and boots. Hair in total disarray, face angelic with a devil smile. He had the most incredible smell. Cloves, marijuana, and sandalwood. Permeated everything, drove me crazy. I'm a whore when it comes to sex with men who smell good."

Amber lit another cigarette, hands trembling as she laughed at herself for telling this masturbating weirdo the details about her private life with her tender monster.

"I worshiped him, the fucking dog, but he did give me something special one night," she said, blowing a smoke ring. "We went to a bar for my birthday. I was already high and buzzed. I was getting horny dancing by myself in the corner. I'm dancing and feeling primitive and sexy hot, and I've forgotten who I'm with. Then I smell cloves and sandalwood behind me. He dances behind me, and I'm dying from the heat of wanting him so badly. He kissed my neck, an incredible kiss that made me shudder.

"His smell – God, his smell – his lips, tongue, his hand on my hips as we start grinding. He knows I'm in a bad way, so he walks me to the parking lot, lays me out on the hood of his car, lifts my dress, and puts his tongue deep in my pussy like I'm the fucking Whitesnake chick. I black out for a moment and come back to life because I can smell him again. His lips are on my neck, and my shoulders, and the backs of my ears. I'm exploding with goosebumps and getting wetter and wetter. He goes down on me again, and I moan.

"That fucking man-dog made me moan in public. I feel the front of his shirt, untuck it, and run my fingers inside, feeling the smooth chest I love, smelling him. Jesus, we haven't done anything, and already I'm screaming out every saint's name in holy fucking heaven. All I can do was think about his cock in my cunt."

Amber took a deep breath.

Remembering sex with Kevin always manifested into real physical pleasure. There was now a tingling in her groin. She shifted her weight and began to piece together the rest of that night.

"So, we go back to my place. I open the door, and Kevin's best friend Alan is standing there in my apartment. And I'm like, who the fuck cares? I'm too horny and stoned to give a shit, and I'm going to fuck my boyfriend regardless. I went to freshen up. Kevin and Alan were in the living room whispering something about a surprise for my birthday. I had no idea what it was. I didn't care what it was.

"I only wanted Kevin to fuck me, and I wanted unbridled, hardcore, and naughty shit too. My heart's beating like crack whore at a track meet, right? But just for fun, I paraded into the center of the living room with my dress hiked up over my ass – I never wore panties when I went out – and I bend over in front of Kevin and Alan. I look back at them from between my legs, and the two of them were naked on the floor like throw pillows with two huge grins and a pair of growing semis in their hands.

"Incense burned in every corner of the

room, the fire cast an unearthly glow on the bodies of these two guys, Eiffel 65 played trashy, sexy Euro trance beats, and so I took off my dress and danced for them in my heels. I pranced and preened. I dipped, and boy, did I shimmy. I slithered in an arcing snake crawl back and forth across the floor, offering them a long good look at my opened ass and pussy, which I caressed with my fingertips. I flipped my ass around and continued to finger myself for them, making my flesh ripple with chill bumps and my pink nipples pop up and perk.

"I flung my shoes to Kevin, who was nodding at me to fuck Alan, looking up at me with his big brown eyes and bright red face. He wasn't bad looking, and he usually smelled nice – he had great skin though. A nice lean frame and a normal-sized cock that was as hard as a lead pipe.

"He jumped when I poked his prick with my finger, but he nearly had a heart attack when I squatted over him like an insect, moving my wet pussy back and forth directly over his dick like a pendulum. Then I straddled him and crawled up the length of his body, over his torso, his neck and face, and stopped before my grinning boyfriend, who was beckoning me with his finger.

"My cunt is right over Alan's mouth, so I slowly bend forward, my head now between Kevin's legs, and I take my boyfriend's cock into my mouth. I felt Alan's hot breath on my slit, and it sent shivers through me. He made me jump the moment I felt his hands spread my ass just before his tongue went spelunking in my pussy. I groaned as I sucked Kevin's hard dick, and then those two naughty boys swapped places. At this time, I had no idea just how far we would take this. I didn't care really.

"I wanted them both now, and I always get my way. So, I was fondling Alan's balls and suckling his prick as Kevin was tongue tapping around my asshole, lightly in and out of my cunt, and back to my asshole.

"What he was doing to me back there – Christ, it was incredible. All I felt was a warm, velvety piece of flesh caressing my lips and clit and rosebud, all three of which throbbed while I sucked on his best friend's sweet little cock. I wondered if I would feel guilty when this was all over, which was fast approaching. I'd always been curious about being with two men, but I didn't expect it would happen tonight, not even on my birthday. I didn't want it to end now that it was actually happening.

"Alan and Kevin got up, and I looked at the two men sweating in front of me. The first told me to lie on my back. I obeyed. The second told me to close my eyes. I obeyed. I felt one hot tongue probing my cunt and the other tasting the flesh of my arms, thighs, neck, and nipples.

"I felt hands lift and then part my legs before my horny boys took turns dipping into my unbelievably wet pussy. I opened wider for Alan, who was earnestly drinking me, and then exploring me with one, two, then three fingers. Kevin was now rubbing his cock over my neck, my cheeks, my mouth, under my jaw – he parted my mouth with the tip and slipped it between my lips.

"This is how we three spent the next half-hour, with the boys switching places every few minutes or so. The urges for release were brutal and painful, and so far beyond my experience that I can't make sense of anything. Alan was suckling my clit, which was hard and swollen and throbbing.

"I tasted Kevin's pre-cum. He let out a small cry and pulled out of me. Alan stopped too. At this point, I was almost crying from a sublime agony – nothing in my life felt more delicious.

"I looked at my boys, and my whole body began to shake. I was teetering upon heights I'd never known and they did nothing but stare at me. When Alan lay on his back, Kevin pulled me up and guided me over to his friend's cock, positioning my pussy in the right spot for me to slide down on his prick. I'm so wet and open now, and I take it in to the hilt. I lean forward and start to move in circles. He moans and shudders the faster I rock and roll.

"I'm in heat as I spin and he pumps, and I wanted to do this all night. But I was going crazy now, sliding around it faster and pumping up and down in it harder. I suddenly felt Kevin move behind me, pinching my nipples and pressing me forward, coating his fingers with clear slick glide.

"His fingers slicked the rim of my ass, coating inside and outside, and then the head of his cock. As Alan moved inside my pussy, the tip of Kevin's prick began to knock at the aperture of my ass, probing it inside just before slowly pushing through.

"I relaxed my muscles for Kevin, his cock filling my pelvis as Alan filled my cunt. And there's me, rocking back and forth between them, my mind spinning, body reeling, my heart pounding, my body sweating. I can hardly breathe. Their pace quickened. I moaned from the waves of impending climax, feeling the ebb and flow, the rising crests, all coming at me in fast shallow waves.

"I let out a deeper groan when the waves recede, but then Kevin went rigid. He began pumping my ass with long, slow strokes. Alan went rigid beneath me, and when he screamed from his release, so did Kevin, balls deep inside my ass, his body shuddering and shaking as he fell across my back. Alan was filling my pussy with his cum and jerking with too much pleasure.

"And then, when the waves returned for me, I began to flail and thrash my body, unable to control the shaking and the quivering, and the silent scream as I imploded with spasms so intense that I wept uncontrollable until they finally subside.

"Kevin was a fucking dog for breaking up with me, but he did give me something no one else will ever give me."

Amber sighed.

"Look what I've done to myself," she said, an unbearable wetness between her legs. Turning to the stranger, she told him, "Gimme your coat a sec. It won't take long."

When the man obliged, Amber yanked the coat over her legs and diddled herself to orgasm.

The man smiled.

"I'm Ted, by the way."

"Fuck you, Ted — I always go for two, so shut up and let me dance."

Ted nodded that he did get it.

He kept quiet as Amber got hers once again.

*

Meghan finishes reading. Closes the folder and sighs.

"I might want your cock in my ass tonight, Joss," she says, tucking the folder into a duffle bag behind her seat. "And I can't take any more of this teasing bullshit baby step reading."

"Wanna talk about it?" I ask, grinning.

"No, I really don't, and fuck you, right in the ear."

Meghan crosses her arms. Stares out her window.

"I'm not normally a 'cunt' kind of dirty talking-reading gal. You know? I think it might be my favorite word. It sounds deliciously taboo when a woman uses it, don't you think? I hate it when men use it—they make it sound like a joke or a threat. I like a man to say the word 'pussy' though. Boy, do I like the sound of that."

I smile as we leave the Blue Ridge Parkway.

We pass a road sign that says Cherokee is three miles away. Up ahead, I see hotels and flatter land, and civilization.

The late afternoon is fading into early dusk. My heart is pounding, and I don't know why.

*

Rolling Blackouts

> *Your face is lit like a sexy star as you climb. Sliding and nuzzling my neck, my navel, my cunt—I feel you linger. Return to me then. Retrace your steps to my mouth and kiss me, your tongue tapping my flesh like little footsteps, bringing the taste and smell of me to my lips. Your sweet breath, spicy with musk, fills me with thoughts of obsession and fucking. I say yes to them as I open for you. A singular thrust, a long slow-burning slide deep inside my sudden silence. My sweat protracted, I rise upward as you retreat from my depths, from my slippery sheath, from my translucence. My breath quickens, my mind roils, my tears flow—oh, what you do to make me weep as I seep.*
>
> —Simone Simon, from *Precipice*

WE CHECK IN AND HEAD TO OUR ROOM. I get our belongings from the car, and after I leave the parking lot, I stop to watch my girl. She's slinking up the set of stairs in a sexy sway that makes my heart climb up Solsbury Hill as my cock goes boom-boom-boom.

My vision blurs from watching without blinking.

The memory of how we began this morning is a blur. What was the first thing we said to each other? I don't remember. All I want to remember is her ass in those pants.

Damn, what a woman.

When she walks into the room, I grab our bags from the car and do the same. I get into the room and put my arms around her. She touches my leather jacket with a melancholy smile, a crying on the inside, Send in the Clowns kind of smile.

"What's wrong, baby?" I ask.

Meghan looks at me with Japanese anime water eyes. "Let's get showered and dressed," she says, running her hands on my arms. "Gary and Carol are expecting us. Hey, let's end this week with a bang and an earth-shattering scream," she says in my ear, sucking my lobe and reaching for her purse. "Here, take this," she orders, handing me a tiny white baby tooth-sized pill. She pops one into her mouth and grimaces as she swallows. "I'll give you a second one when we head out—drop the first one and join me in the shower."

"Is this E?" I ask.

Meghan grins. "Silly boy—Gary and Carol gave me some of their pharmaceutical grade stuff last night," she tells me, peeling out of her top and bottom, unhooking her bra, and stepping out of her panties. "This'll help us do things to make the legislature of this fine state pass new blue laws prohibiting it ever after."

"Why two pills"

"The first cleans you out like no enema or diuretic you know—the second one will kick the first one in and make you roll your brains out for hours and hours," she says. "So, how about you get out of those clothes and take a nice long shower with me? We'll be taking another in less than twenty minutes, I promise."

I am surprised when the pill does exactly what she says it will. My colon's been gutted like a Halloween pumpkin. The cleansing effects are beyond rejuvenating—I feel as if I've been opened, prepared for ritual. I begin my second shower with a mind in other realms. And I am so thirsty I drink shower water for two minutes without coming up for air. It's more water than I've had all day.

My thoughts are reeling and I begin to phase in and out of the present.

Hell, I don't even notice Meghan leaving the shower, turning on the hair dryer, sitting on the toilet, leaving the bathroom, and coming back to do her hair and makeup. Usually, a hot shower is the most relaxing thing I know. I like to lie down on the tub floor and let the water hiss over me like a waterfall. I love the white noise, the beautiful drone.

Boy, this pill is some fucking trippy little monster.

I'm almost dreading the second one. My heart pumping, my throat tightening, my face flushing, I get out and towel off, and then I drink more water. I piss twice. I get dressed for a semi-formal evening out—black shoes, black pants, and long sleeved shirt, skinny red tie.

When we leave the room, I take pill number two.

"I love you, Joss," Meghan tells me. "Try to remember that tonight, and after."

And after, she said.

Oh, if I'd had the clarity to pick up on those two words.

I want to say something, but I can't stop sucking my teeth—I am hot and cold, hot and cold. My clothes feel so good rubbing against my skin, and then the wave passes. I'm back to a state of feeling almost normal, slightly high with heightened senses.

"I love you so much I can hardly breathe," I tell her.

Meghan laughs. "That's the drug talking, baby," she says, giving me a sip from her water bottle. "You've never loved me or anybody that much."

I slow blink my eyes. "This is weird stuff, baby—it comes in at you like these waves of tingles everywhere. How come you look so normal?"

She shrugs. "Maybe mine hasn't kicked in," she replies. "Here, drink up."

"I gotta pee again," I tell her, unzipping and unpacking, pissing into a bush on the side of the building. I sip the water and shudder—my hair's still a bit wet.

I say nothing more as we head into the unknown of early evening.

I'm not an intuitive person.

I have no gift for sensing what's coming or going, let alone what's happening around me.

On more than one occasion, my inability to pick up social clues has been the bane of my existence. I've been accused of being an insensitive asshole, a pathetically dense frat-boy, a self-absorbed prick, a hot autistic savant—hell, at the start of this trip, Meghan jokingly snapped and called me Beautiful Mind.

But this drug I'm on—**boom.**

My awareness is sharpened to so fine a point that I feel everything around me, I see sounds and taste colors, and I hear textures. As we walk to Carol and Gary's, I am filled with this overwhelming sense of impending danger. Of course, it also can be drug-induced paranoia, which is par for the course, I suppose.

One thing I will say is how sexualized I am feeling—that coupled with all those hours on the Parkway, and I don't recall a time I've ever felt so horny.

I absently stroke my crotch as we walk by fountains and floral displays. Past the lounge and restaurant, through the lobby to the atrium. We stroll past the garden by the swimming pool and make our way to the platinum suite, a large detached dwelling on the western side of the property.

We reach a gated fence and private walkway.

Meghan punches a code into the keypad, opens the door, and leads me down a gravel path to the apartment at the bottom of the hill. The twilight is so crisp and cold I stumble as I gaze upward, oblivious to everything else. I'm still looking skyward when she lets go of my hand to hug someone waiting for us.

Smelling clove cigarette smoke, I turn to see Gary ushering Meghan into the suite through the back door. The strangest look passes between them—it's the look of secrets being kept.

"You alright, son?" Gary asks, tossing away his butt with a bemused chuckle. "Looks like the pills are hitting you. Carol's rolling her ass around the carpets and rugs like a cat in heat. I'm feeling a tingle, but it'll be some time before I start howling at the moon. I've got some water in the tiki bar over there."

After Gary tosses me a bottle, which I slurp down immediately, he stands back a few feet and looks at me. He doesn't speak for several minutes, which means ten or sixty—my sense of time is akimbo. Gary smiles as he embraces me, and then again as he holds me at arm's length. He takes me by the chin and turns my face. Then he walks around me a few times, nodding to himself and humming his approval, the fingers of one hand lightly grazing my collarbone and shoulders as he circles and studies me.

When we're facing each other again, I notice he's not nearly as tall as he seems to be. He's shorter than me—I'm no giant, but I am six-one in my bare feet, and he's wearing boots. Taking my hand, Gary leads me to the bar stools and sits in the one beside me.

Who the fuck IS this guy?

"You know, before Carol and I were married, I was living with this guy named Greg. We were best friends, did everything together. Well, we almost did. We fooled around when we got high together, but that's it. He wanted to do more, but I didn't. I liked women more, and he hated that about me. Didn't understand why I couldn't switch between both. It wasn't until after he left that I understood what he was trying to tell me. It was the 70s and everyone was fucking everyone—you remember Carol's story.

"Anyway, Greg made me realize how people are sometimes thrown together for a reason, a season, or a lifetime. What I learned from his absence was how keen the sting of missed opportunities felt. Know what I'm talking about?"

I tell myself I do know exactly what he's talking about. And then I tell him the same thing, and all I want is for him to understand that I do.

With a shudder, I touch his arm. "It could be that I'm about to start rolling my ass off, Gary, but I feel a real connection to you. I've been trying to figure out what it is I feel about you and Carol, and I honestly don't know yet. I'm just glad I'm here with you in this moment, Gary—whatever the reason or the season, I want you to know I'm grateful for what you and Carol did for Meghan and me. We're closer than we have been, and I can't wait to hear what you guys have to say."

"Did Meghan tell you the truth?"

Again, I touch Gary's arm. "Yes, she did," I reply. "I told her I wasn't angry that she enlisted two therapists—we obviously needed help. We still won't be able to afford your couples retreat center though. I went online and saw the prices."

Gary pats my hand. "Joss, we have to put a cost to what we do—otherwise, people who seek our help wouldn't believe we were legitimate. As I told you, we assess couples on an individual basis and then design the program that suits their specific needs—as Carol and I have done for you and Meghan. We started doing this over thirty years ago, so we have a good idea about the people we invite to the ranch."

"Man, you guys look amazing—you don't look old at all. How do you do it?"

Gary laughs. "We do what we love, we indulge passions to the fullest, we keep fit and eat healthy, and we do not limit our experiences—not as individuals, not as a couple, not as a man, not as a woman, not as business partners, not as friends. We keep our minds and our hearts as open as the mountain vistas. Carol and I wanted to help you open your mind and heart tonight, so we gave Meghan those happy pills."

Taking a deep breath, I say, "And for that I thank you."

"We use MDMA at our facility as part of our therapy for new couples, especially during the first week of the program," Gary explains. "It's not the Ecstasy street drug, even though the effects are similar. Euphoria, diminished anxiety, a sense of intimacy—all the good stuff and none of the bad stuff."

My mind is starting to reel. "I should be angry with you, Carol, and Meghan, you three planning and plotting without my knowing it," I confess. "I'm not, but I should be."

"That's good, Joss—we just wanted you to feel comfortable and relaxed," Gary tells me. "This is an important step for your relationship, you know."

I close my eyes with a lazy smile. "It is an important step, but I'm no dummy," I say. "I knew what was going to happen tonight. Well, I suspected you had ulterior motives as we went through your folder, getting horned up from listening to all that talk about fucking, and then Meghan reading that story."

The wind blows sweet night mountain air. A dog barks in the distance. I don't know how long the silence is, but it stretches outward like a wave of electric energy, humming a rolling heat that returns and loops.

"Have you fucked Meghan yet?"

Gary laughs. "I was wondering when you'd ask me that question—do you really want an answer?"

"Yes, I do—and I won't be angry if you have."

"I know that," he tells me, "but I haven't had the privilege of fucking her."

"But she stayed with you and Carol last night."

"Slept on the sleeper sofa," Gary reassures me. "It turns you on to think of me fucking her," he says. "You confessed to a lot of things last night, which admittedly turned me on, my dear boy. But Carol and I have a system in place that precludes us taking advantage of you before we officially invite you into the fold."

"Are you doing that tonight? Inviting us into the fold? We can't afford it, Gary."

"Yes, you can," he says, getting up. "I'm starting to feel more than a few tingles myself. Aren't you?"

"I've had a hard cock for an hour or so," I confess. "What else is in those pills?"

Gray chuckles. "Proprietary ingredients—let's just say you'll have that tool primed and ready for anything over the next few hours," he tells me. "Oh, you'll feel like you're floating in dream, a very lucid, very wet dream. We should head into the suite and see what the girls have cooked up for us."

"But I'm feeling strange—like I'm on a boat."

Gary ignores me. "I'd imagine Carol's giddy about tonight—let me tell you something, bubba. My wife's got a sweet, tight little pussy. Oh, that snug twat's a miracle fit for men like us."

"Men like us?" I ask, feeling another rushing wave.

I feel like I am lost in a lucid dream.

And I suddenly want to keep exploring it.

Gary puts my hand on his crotch. "Men like us," he repeats, gently squeezing my erection. "We both have a solid piece of equipment, although yours has some real girth to it—fuck." He moves in closer to me. "Carol and I believe the human body is capable of so much more pleasure if it's shared with those you trust and love. We so want to trust and love you and your precious, precious Meghan.

Heterosexual, homosexual—there's only bisexual, my dear boy. Oh, there are general sexual proclivities for this and that—male and female must procreate, after all. But there are pleasures we can give and receive that exist outside of creating life."

My heart is pounding as Gary moves even closer.

I feel his breath on my neck as he speaks low into my ear. "Joss, what seems taboo is merely someone else imposing their rules on your life," he says. "Sex binds us, connects us, but it also sets us free. It liberates. Both of you no longer need to live lives of duality and lies. Meghan no longer needs to be ashamed of her insatiable urges and you no longer need wonder whether you're gay or not. Limiting your sexual nature or the nature of one you love causes more strife than you can imagine. Carol and I are going to help you celebrate, instead of punish, each other. You both have earned tonight, so roll into that roll you feel, and don't be afraid to explore the unknown with us. Carol and I are here to guide you."

Gary kisses my cheek. "You did read the book I lent you last night."

"Of course, I did," I lie to him, not knowing if it really is a lie.

Did I read the book?

No, I didn't, and I don't care.

He embraces me. "Then none of this should come as a shock, my dear boy."

*

I am rolling in and out of strange waves, the ebb and tide of co-mingling drug effects. I'm hot and cold, barely and wide-awake, hallucinating and lucid, pliable and horny and open.

"Is this my education, Gary?" I ask.

He doesn't answer. He takes me by the hand and leads me to a dark room with dim lighting and cushions thrown everywhere. From the speakers I hear trance music, the beat-beat-beat of a steady pulsating drum track and synth chords that knead the melody with a massaging, sensual touch. Mounted to the walls are large flat screens playing hardcore porn videos for different erotic tastes.

> *My wife fucks other men when I'm not around. She doesn't know that I know how many or how often—a shitload and frequently would be the appropriate answers. What a fucking cunt, the poor dear. Now, I'm not a cruel man, but I do have my limits. It's time I teach the bitch a lesson. See, she thinks I'm on my way to work, but I'm about to turn the car around and head back home—what a surprise this'll be.*

Gary hands me a bottle of water, which I drain in three gulps.

He hands me another and tells me to keep watching the video about the man driving home to surprise his philandering wife.

> *When I caught my wife cheating the first time, the cock inside her belonged to my best friend. Ah, that was a*

> *sight. And the sounds they made, the coital facial contortions of pleasure—not that sexy, although I'm certain the God Priapus and Goddess Pussynova would've begged to differ. All I know is seeing them together sent such a shock of black electricity to my brain that I spent several long minutes tennis balling between states of euphoric horniness and ecstatic homicidal jealousy—what a fucking rush. After I watched them fuck, I fainted from the exquisite pain of agonizing arousal and jealousy at having witnessed another man plunging his cock deep inside my wife's round ass.*

Gary is standing behind me whispering in my ear as the narration plays. His voice is hypnotic—I swear to God, if I didn't know any better, I'd believe anything he told me. As I watch the screen, I let the images and words inside me.

I feel intoxicated and electric.

I feel as if I am slipping the surly bonds of my body to find a new home for my astral soul. Gary tells me I'm a husband in a broken marriage, and I don't doubt him.

When he asks me if I am married, I say yes.

At least, I think I do.

It doesn't matter who I am or what I'm saying, I am remade as another man.

My mind is spinning so fast I can't keep track of my thoughts. I can't keep track of the order of events—my short term memory is in a constant state of hiccuping and image-skipping.

I don't know when I took off my clothes either, but I am suddenly standing naked beside Gary, now rubbing and massaging my body with scented oils, caressing every inch of my tingling skin.

"Beautiful and perfect," he says, asking me to bend and twist. "You are a god—wait 'til Carol sees."

Carol.

Do I know a Carol?

Feeling luxurious and sexual and thick with desire, I ask about the woman playing my wife. And I ask about the men playing the other characters. I ask about the scenes we're filming—*are we filming?*—and how long the takes are. I have no idea if I actually put sound to my thoughts.

"Do we get a rehearsal, Gary?"

"This is the only rehearsal," he says, chuckling low. "Watch what's playing on screen, listen to the story, imagine yourself as a husband who'll do anything to make his wife happy."

> *With the adulterous deed unmasked, what else was there to do but fuck with them both? I reached out and traced the outline of Allen's red prominence, a rather thick protruding one that motions up and down in time with his pulse. He moved a step backward, but I grabbed his arm and threw it at my dear wife wringing her hands next to him. Her face was ashen. She had her robe around her, but untied, the gap exposed her*

> *breasts from time to time. I smelled their smells, their sweat and heat. 'You should've told me. I want it too.'*

Gary leads me into another room. I am hypnotized now—I am beginning to believe this is my life and Meghan is my wife who's cheating on me with my best friend Allen.

I am leaving my body.

I am leading another man's life.

*

I've left a road slick with morning rain, that I've parked my car in the drive, that I've opened the door to my house. Three-story stucco. Several thousand square feet. Nice neighborhood. Allen may be here. He lives next door. I walk into the kitchen from the garage and hear the shower running upstairs.

Is there an upstairs?

Ah, yes, and I smell incense burning, shocks of sandalwood and other strange Eastern spices. Strange trance music plays on the stereo so loud I can barely hear the voices beyond my bedroom as I walk toward the shower room. The lone voice of my wife humming and moaning—and other voices adding their contributions to the symphony of groaning and moaning.

My hands are shaking. I feel crazy lust, my depraved thoughts hot and dark with heady sinful desire.

My wife and I don't make love any more, not since I've discovered her exotic appetites, which I strive to satisfy. It's comfortable and familiar, and the possibilities are endless now that being reduced to an animal is part of our daily routine. Maybe Allen and I need to fuck each other today. It could lead us all to new heights of kink, connection, pleasure, and freedom. I'm broader and stronger than Allen is, so I could force myself on him.

I've got a bigger cock—and it would be such a pleasure to take him like that.

It would be a pleasure for him too.

Allen—do I even know an Allen?

Maybe I do, maybe I don't—I'm not all that interested in his fucking name, even if he's my best friend. I am already naked and hard as I walk into the bathroom and head to the steam room behind it.

I told you our house was huge.

I open the door and go inside. There is little steam, but plenty of hissing warm water and mist in the air. The room is a wide square, big enough to hold a room of people.

Right now, I am expecting to find only three.

To my surprise, there are eight people here. Two women, including my wife, and six men, including me. Three men surround her on all sides. One man is sitting in the far corner taking pictures of them and masturbating. My wife is painted like a whore, dark eyes, and bright red lipstick.

The three men surrounding her, including Allen, are rubbing

their hard pricks on her body as they feel her up, kiss and lick her body—I believe Allen is pumping her ass with his cock, but it's hard to see. The second woman I don't know.

She's watching them and telling them what to do for the masturbating man taking pictures.

The other two men are strangers to me.

My wife starts sucking on both of them—first, the muscle guy's dick, and then, the lean guy's dick. Allen is still fucking her ass from behind. The sight is unbearable hot, and I can't help myself when I start stroking my cock.

The strange woman sees me. She stands up and walks around the foursome, as if on cue, and sidles up to me. She's got the biggest bounciest tits I've ever seen—the next thing I know, I'm getting ready to slide my hard dick between them. "I'm Carol," she says, kneeling, "but you already know that, don't you?"

Do I know Carol—I think I do, but it's like a woman from a dream.

Am I dreaming?

Her tits are like round, perky gourds, soft as dough, nipples dark as red wine.

God, can she suck a cock.

I wonder how long this had been planned. It's dark and misty and steamy. I'm sweating and hard, and I order Carol to push her big tits together and make a coozie for me. She spits into the fold, and I slide my prick upward.

As I fuck and slide, I tell her to open her mouth and drink my piss. Carol laughs and does what I tell her to do. I unleash a gushing stream into her waiting mouth, which she delights in drinking and gargling.

And over there, Allen and the boys are taking turns with Meghan. The former still takes her from behind as the latter two take turns face-fucking my wife. Over growls and groans, I can hear Meghan's familiar throaty, hoarse fuck-me voice. "In my ass—Jesus…yes."

Carol slaps my ass. "Hey, eyes on me, stud. Fuck my tits."

"Fuck you," I tell her.

Carol smiles. "You will."

So, I watch my cock glide between her breasts, wet beads form like water on a well-waxed car. She groans and says, "Holy fuck, what a big boy you are. My big boy, what a big boy you are—fuck Mommy's titties, my big boy."

Meghan coos with an orgasm, mist and splashing, water spraying. Allen jerks wildly before going rigid, suddenly stopping as he comes in her ass, pulling out for the other two men to suck and lick dry and clean.

My wife gets on all fours and orders one of the men to suck the cum from her ass. She orders Allen to lick the other man's cock. She moans even more when Allen finishes sucking the rest of his semen from her bright pink, slicked, and fuck-swollen hole. My wife pushes Allen back with her foot and offers herself to the other two men.

"Take your turn, boys," she says, wiggling. "Two at a time."

They each move forward, one slips his dick into the top of her widening asshole from behind, the other sliding it in beneath her with Allen's eager assistance, pulling her up and back as she kneels on the tiles. Her eyes are half slits, mouth opening and closing like a fish, perfect tits jiggling and bouncing. Allen pinches her nipples and circles her clit with his pussy-wet fingers. She moans louder as she bounces until an almost inaudible yes escapes her, which Allen soon fills with a slowly stiffening half-limp-but-rejuvenated cock.

Carol pulls away from me.

She gets to her feet and slaps me in the face, kisses me as she spanks my ass.

Then, she walks over to the foursome against the glass wall. She grabs Allen by the back of his hair and points him to the masturbating man in the corner. She pulls Meghan away from the other men and hands her a thick dildo with long strips at the base. She slaps one of the men in the face and grabs him by the back of the head, pulling it back hard enough to make him wince.

Carol turns back to me with a smile. "This one's been a naughty boy," she says. "Allen, quit sucking Gary's cock and help Mommy punish this very bad boy." Her hand gripping the targeted man's hair, Carol yanks it. "Open up—there's a good boy," she says, spitting in his mouth and moving behind him. Allen steps forward holding his dick, which Carol takes and puts into the open mouth. "Drink this for Mommy—be a big boy."

Allen pisses into the man's mouth, urine filling his face and then spilling down his neck and chest. The man swallows some of it and offers the rest to Carol, who drinks from his opened mouth when Allen falls to his knees beside them.

Meghan takes the dildo whip and begins thrashing them with it. I'm playing with myself, trying to keep from popping off. I never thought I'd enjoy this kind of stuff, let alone seeing Meghan at the center of it like a dominatrix in training. Carol takes a second dildo whip and crams the business end of it into Allen's ass.

My wife crams hers inside one of the two men before she ties their hands behind them with leather binds. I hear whimpering cries erupting into shouts of submission and blissful gratitude as Allen and one of the other two men come over my wife's legs and feet. "Yes," she tells them, turning to the third man.

She takes his throbbing, bouncing cock in her hands, cupping the balls and tugging the skin there. She lightly spans the shaft before she puts her mouth over it, slowly taking his length until she gags. Removing it with a pop, she spits on it and strokes it in long strokes. "On my face, baby boy," she coos.

The man screams and jerks, shooting hot white spunk in thick streams under my wife's chin. Meghan deep throats him once more before squeezing out another shot of pearly white on neck and breasts. Carol removes binds and dildos, and then directs the foursome to the shower in the corner with the masturbating man. He continues taking photographs and shooting video between bouts of jerking off. I watch my wife wash Allen's prick, soaping it up and cleaning it before she moves on to clean the others.

Then I feel the tethers of a whip on my chest.

I grab the whip, force it from Carol's hand, and throw it to the floor. I grab her wrists and pull her to me with a quick jerk. I'm pissed. My hormones raging, what with all this fucking and sucking cocks, and I don't want to be dominated. "I'm not a slave," I tell Carol, whose mocking laugh fills me with fury.

She smiles at me, and in a little girl's voice, she says, "Daddy's gonna punish me, is he? Huh? Big Daddy with his big man daddy cock. C'mon, you pussy, beat this bad girl. I dare you to beat this naughty girl. C'mon, Big Daddy, you better nut up and make me your bitch right now, or I'll make you my pony boy."

Water warm and mist swimming around me.

"On your knees," I shout, feeling dizzy.

Watching my wife in the corner—is she my wife?—making the men hard again.

How is that possible?

I feel licking on my toes, my knees, and thighs.

Carol is giggling and licking and sucking on my skin. She moves her head up and then, suddenly, I feel hands on my ass. I feel a woman's hands on my ass and then as sucking turns into the graying waves of intense pleasure, I feel a mouth on my balls and a slow jabbing finger probing my asshole. She rams her forefinger into me as she sucks my cock.

Then I feel two of her fingers inside me.

I feel electricity between my ass and my cock. She suckles each of my balls, her fingers working my prostate, my forbidden fruits dangling before her open mouth. She gently spins me around, hums as she spreads my cheeks, and plants her tongue deep in my asshole. My mind reels as I shudder from the sensation.

I suddenly hear a man's laugh and the hands of several men on my back and arms.

I hear Carol slopping in my ass trough.

"Fucking pig bitch," I tell her. "Lap it up, little piggy."

Suddenly spun around, the three men pull me to the middle of the room and pin me between them. I feel their erections against my stomach and backside. They start kissing me. Carol picks up the dildo whip and grabs my hair in the back. She yanks my head and says, "You're not ready to be Daddy, are you, pony?"

Meghan says, "Give him to me first."

Her voice is a nether-voice, haunting and siren-like. I feel mechanical and drugged, and suddenly very sad and blue with deep melancholy. Meghan doesn't sound like the name of the woman I married. Does it not?

Wait, am I married?

I feel Carol's whip across my back. I try to stand up, but the other three men keep me pinned. My cock twitches and jerks, swollen from the pain of not having release. And I am in desperate need of it. But I feel like I am no longer a person, my bright crimson prick is filled to bursting with blood, scorching and tortured.

It's as if something is numbing my muscles in my groin.

God, I need to come.

Where's my wife? Where's Allen?

Where's Carol, that minx of kink and leather whips? One of the men kneels in front of the other man, who shoves a dildo deep inside his ass. He's ramming it deep and hard, and then Carol orders them to fuck each other. "Fuck for Mommy, my pony boys—come over here and do it over Mommy, my ponies. Yes, my beautiful bad boys, fuck for Mommy."

As I watch them, I feel cum rising deep inside my balls, in the deepest part beneath my ass, deep in the base of my spinal cord. Meghan is sucking me, and I am holding back, and I am about to lose all sense of my identity.

I suddenly think of catching my mother and father having sex when I was a boy. In my mind I scream at them for leaving me.

For dying on me.

And I want to punish them for it, so I let my wife suck me to the brink as Carol and her boys do their thing. I gently pull Meghan's fingers out of my ass and take her over to a far corner where no one is jerking off, taking pictures, or watching. Call me selfish, but I want my to come inside her without an audience.

I love my wife. I scoop her up in my arms—she's easy to lift—and I tote her to the solitary spot. Behind me, hissing mists and animal sounds, and I ignore them.

Cupping my wife's breasts, I kiss each pink raised nipple before I sink my dick into her sopping wet, crimson hot, unfolded, well-fucked cunt. The points of her tits are harder and deeper red, as I pump her with my cock. Her skin ripples in gooseflesh, her hands and feet begin to shake and quiver.

And when she throws her arms around my neck, she bites my shoulder the harder and faster I fuck her.

"I'm so sorry, Joss, so sorry, please forgive me—I'm so sorry."

Joss? Why is she calling me Joss?

I'm not Joss.

"Hush, my darling," I whisper, my cock vibrating inside her.

I shudder with pleasure and pain as I finally explode. Each pump is filling her with my seed, and I keep screaming and shuddering, every spasm shooting long cords of cum deep into her cunt until she bites the flesh of my shoulder again.

She screams with her own release, her pussy milking more of my hot pearly seed. And it doesn't stop—it doesn't end—and suddenly, I am screaming as I come once again. I scream her name and tell her I love her, feeling my body on the brink of losing consciousness.

As I feel the last drops of my second orgasm extracted, I suddenly forget who I am, where I am, who I am with, why I am there.

I cannot think.

All I can do is feel, and I feel so fucking much right now. I feel lost, filled, angry, purged, connected, and renewed, and my cock is still hard. My swollen cock is still throbbing. I am inside a woman

I call my wife, even though I know she isn't my wife, and I need to explode inside her again.

She begs me to stop, screams for Carol and a man named Gary to help her. I tell her I have what she needs. She buries her face into my neck as I pump her harder, again and again, I can't stop fucking her, and I lift my body, rising up on my haunches, as I shove my rod deep inside her, each thrust harder than the one before it.

"Carol, Gary—help me! Help him!"

My final thrust halts all of my movement. I am frozen in the air, an acrobat gripping his partner, both of them locked in a dance of fucking, arrested in time.

"Don't move," I whisper to her. "Don't move."

Meghan, God bless her, honors my final plea.

I am spinning, spinning, spinning—*fuck, am I spinning and rolling, spinning and rolling.*

And my body swells with the spinning.

She ignores the tears on my face and holds me as the searing nuclear heat of a third orgasm blinds my brain with an exquisite, hyper-explosive release, a jet of blazing fuck-stream as never existed before. And then I black out.

*

Awakening

> *Tender women, you ablaze with love's fire, compensate yourselves now, and do so boldly and unafraid; persuade yourselves that there can exist no evil in obedience to Nature's promptings, that it is not for one man she created you, but to please them all, without discrimination. Let no anxiety inhibit you. It becomes women to surrender themselves to debauchery, and that great man's ideas were not always pure dreams.*
>
> —Marquis de Sade, from *Philosophy in the Bedroom*

I DON'T KNOW WHERE I AM. I'm in some room, an office maybe. I'm handcuffed to a chair. There's a flat screen on the wall to my right playing the same video on repeat, like the channel in your room that advertises the hotel amenities. I watch the screen.

Where the fuck am I?

Cue stock country pastoral music.

Cue sound effects and moving logo of BLUE Studios.

Fade to a wide shot of a ranch in spring as the camera pans Ken Burns style and fades to a tighter shot of a sprawling tract of land with a beautiful panorama in the background. Grazing cows and sheep, goats and ducks, geese and chickens, and horses and cowboys.

Cut to POV shot of a slow ride to the ranch house, a single-story hotel-sized structure that seems to have no end. Cut to inside the lobby, with its flowing fountains and bar, concierge and bellhops. Tour guides leading groups of people.

Fade to happy couples strolling hand in hand on the beautifully kept grounds against the breathtaking backdrop of the Appalachian Mountains. Fade to a long shot of a man and woman in cowboy hats riding horses toward the camera. Quick cut, a tighter frame shot of the two climbing down and then giving over the reins to a rancher who leads the horses toward the stables.

The man in the cowboy hat looks at the camera and says, "I'm Gary Rider, licensed sex therapist, best-selling author, successful businessman, and lifelong horse-lover."

The woman in the cowboy hat looks at the camera and says, "I'm Dr. Carol Rider, licensed sex therapist, psychiatrist, couples counselor, best-selling author, successful businesswoman, and lifelong horse-lover." Cut to a two shot of Gary and Carol standing arm in arm as they look to the camera and say, "Welcome to Blue Mountain Ranch, Holistic Health Facility, and Couples Retreat."

More shots of the ranch and land around it.

Shots of happy couples walking, riding, fishing, doing chores, taking classes, attending workshops. Interviews with couples before and after their week-long therapy program.

Cut to a frank discussion about sex in the main hall—Carol is lecturing a large group of couples attending the retreat.

"Women and men are different creatures. Physically, emotionally, intellectually—they might as well come from two separate planets. The reason why relationships fail comes down to what makes men and women different. At Blue Mountain, we help our couples accept those differences through honesty, trust, intimacy, and sex—LOTS of it."

The group applauds wildly as the screen fades to Gary discussing their most recent expansion, a successful line of erotic videos and books developed for new couples coming to the Ranch by couples who have successfully completed the program.

Cut to Carol speaking to a different audience.

"We strive to show human sexuality as the dynamic biological force we believe it to be. In doing that over time, we amassed a huge case history of stories and session transcripts that we were able to retool for the benefit of new couples coming to the retreat. With the permission of our most successful couples, we share the private erotic lives of real people in real situations for real healing and real connections to foster real and lasting intimacy. Ladies and gentleman, I am proud to present BLUE, our award winning line of erotic books, stories, games, and films."

There's a montage of various activities, including swimming and aerobics, movie night and talent show night, group therapy, counseling sessions, people arguing then crying and hugging, people laughing, people making love, and ending with quick snapshots of couples giving testimonials—

—all of them glowing and positive.

Where the fuck am I?

A woman enters the room. She grabs a remote from the desk and presses a button to mute the sound. She's petite, mocha-skinned, and striking—those eyes are a shade of green that can't be real. She's familiar, but I don't know why. She sits on the edge of her desk and thumbs through a manila folder.

"Tarot. Astrology. Lucky dice. A rabbit's foot. A monkey's paw. A stinky T-shirt worn on special occasions. People put their faith into talismans because they hope Fortune will reward them for their devotion. Tell me, Joss Parker, did Fortune bring you to Blue Mountain Ranch, or was it random chance?"

I try to speak, but there's cotton in my mouth.

I can't think straight, and I can't swallow.

"Not a chance you were a threat to your life and to the lives of others? Is there a chance for that, Joss Parker? Hmm? Or maybe a chance that you were so tweaked on MDMA, GHB, Sildenafil citrate—that's Viagra, by the way—Rohypnol, and good ol' alcohol. I have the toxicology report right here if you want me to show it to you. Joss, talk to me."

But I can't talk to her—I'm thinking about how shitty Meghan treated me. About how fucked-up and numb I feel. How surreal the days have passed through my head, as if I've been dreaming them by. WHAT THE HELL? Carol and Gary had me RUFFIED, for fuck's sake. All this takes center stage in my brain until, quite suddenly, I hear the snapping of fingers right in my ears. Left to right, left to right.

All I can think of is the first girl I ever loved.

Her name was Simone too.

Simone.

"Joss Parker, open your eyes."

I never knew emotional pain like that before—first love kills you when it's over.

"Joss Parker, what's my name?"

I never allowed myself to get close to anyone else like that again, not even to Meghan, which might explain why I didn't really mind her infidelity as much as I should have. It's why I left her and never looked back until she called out of the fucking BLUE—well, she's getting her revenge now, isn't she? I'm blacking out again.

"Joss, look at me—no, eyes open. Fuck."

My eyes roll in the back of my head, and I lose consciousness.

Simone, dear Simone, deliver me from evil.

*

Simone, I have a confession to make. I often speak your name aloud so that I may hear its sound. I don't think it's a conscious gesture, not completely. It just happens, and when it happens, to say it consumes me is a half-truth. It ravages me to say it. Simone, it's a small prayer, a whisper of hope in a dream—like a chant in the forest primeval, a Goddess of the Earth brought to life in the Now—within me like some new heartbeat. Simone, I ache to say it, as I ache to hold you and whisper it in your ear. And the sighs I long to hear escape from your lips—and the hush of desire, like the ultimate shudder of release as I come inside you. And through you, Simone, I am a man remade, and so, I say it again and again and again. Simone, to hear it spoken, as an echoing path toward secret hollows, it is the music of love and lust and silence. To see in reflected in your eyes, the gaze of passion never wavering, as my body rocks in beautiful agony when you move beneath me, pulling the ropes of my essence out slowly, one chord of liquid heat at a time, until I am spent, and all that is left to me is the sound of your name. Simone, broken into parts, its syllabic essence is sim and one. In some cultures, sim and ona, a beat added to make the sacred number of syllables three, ending at the beginning of the alphabet with the letter for Alpha, for One, for Ona, the graceful one, or for Oona, for the unity of one coupled to Sim or Si, which means yes. Yes, Simone, I am a foolish man and must submit myself to you lest I be dismantled, disintegrated, destroyed. Your light to a lesser man's eyes would leave him a blind fool, for only a lesser man stare directly into her brilliance, her turbulence. I laugh and welcome that death, should you wish it. For yours is the blaze of divinity, and I am merely a mortal spark doomed to fizzle in a moment.

*

"Simone," I hear myself say, the sound of my voice waking me up. "I was dreaming of you."

My eyes are closed, so I don't see the surprise on her face, a truth she will later confess to me after everything else begins to fall a-fucking-apart.

"Here, drink this," she tells me.

There's a glass of water at my lips. I drink, and cough when it goes down my windpipe, but I drink more until the glass is empty. I clear my throat. "I don't believe in luck," I say, my voice scratchy. "I only believe that hell hath no fury than that of a woman scorned."

Simone smiles. "So, you're not a complete idiot."

"Why am I here?"

"I already told you—Dr. Rider had you Baker Acted," she says. "You are under the care of Dr. Rider until she releases you. That means you will be here a long time, my friend."

"Gary and Carol tricked me."

Simone laughs. "No doubt they did, but they're the bosses," she says. "For the time being, you and I are going to be the best of friends. You're going to listen to me and do everything I say over the next few days—otherwise, you'll make things harder than they need to be. All you have to do is learn your lessons and do what I tell you to do."

"What if I don't?"

Simone sighs. "You'd be a naughty boy then, wouldn't you?"

"And naughty boys get punished?"

"You have no idea," she says, gripping my arm. "Carol will make your life a living hell. She's giving you a chance that no other cockmonger gets—"

"Cockmonger? What's that?"

"Potential studs for the BLUE films," Simone replies.

"What do you mean for the BLUE films? I'm not a porn actor."

Simone studies my face. "You honestly have no idea, do you?"

My head is pounding. "No, I don't," I tell her, making a move to rub my temples. The handcuffs keeping my hands right where they are. "Do you hog tie all new guests?"

"Only until I get you processed and cleaned," Simone says. "You need a hot shower, boy. You are filthy and you reek."

I feel tears in my eyes. I turn my head away, too weak to keep the water from spilling down my face. "I'm not supposed to be here," I tell her, unable to wipe the evidence of my fear and frustration. "They drugged me. I was brought here against my will."

Simone takes my chin in her hand. "And you think I'm not," she whispers, gazing at me with piercing intensity, her brown eyes searching mine for a sign of life. "Shut up, do what I say, and you'll stay in Carol's good graces. It doesn't matter what you want—you are going to be their golden boy for next year's batch of adult films. It's the first year BLUE films will be shown at chain movie theaters for limited engagements. You fuck this up, and you'll be sent to the stables with the rest of the ponies for a very long time. I'm going to take off the handcuffs. You're going to bathe, and then, after I take you to your room, you're going to eat and rest."

"But why—"

Simone slaps my face. "You get this one chance," she says, her teeth set and voice hard. "Normally, I wouldn't give a shit, but even I have a soft spot for hard-luck cases. If you shut your mouth and do as I say, things will be okay. If you ask too many questions, if you push your luck with me or with Carol and Gary, you'll have to start at the bottom and work your way back to the same fucking spot."

*

It's after midnight, in the witching hour part of morning.

It's cold.

I stand naked and alone in the wet lawn outside my tiny cubicle-like dorm room.

I shiver as I stand there in my bare feet, my breath fogging the space around me as I take my air bath. In the distance, I see the shadows of mountains below a night sky of stars and cosmic dust. As much as I want to believe this is a dream, I know it's not.

I've seen the film I made with Meghan the night we got to Cherokee. I've never seen anything so base, so debauched. I wept for an hour after I watched it with Simone. I wept for another hour after she brought me to my tiny room and left.

I feel like I've been orphaned all over again.

How did I get here?

Simone tells me I'll be doing another film later this week. She tells me I need to do more than just make the film. She tells me I need to take my performance to the next level this time.

As if I had any control over the previous one—Jesus, I don't remember what I did that night. I mean, I understand now, having seen what I did. My ability to have multiple orgasms in quick succession is a rare gift apparently.

I didn't believe her until I saw the footage myself.

That I'm so young and healthy, that I'm hypersensitive to the proprietary drug cocktail they kept pumped in my system, that I'm so honest in front of the camera, that I have one of those penises that looks big flaccid or hard—apparently, I'm the IT guy.

I don't want to be their IT guy.

I don't want to make another film for them.

I want to go back to my apartment and my life, and I want to pretend like Meghan never called me. Pretend like I never heard from her. Like I never knew her, never loved her, never forgave all her sins against me. In my mind, I keep going over my week with Ben, and I keep wishing I'd never left the safety of his barn.

And then my mind goes back to the sight of Meghan fucking Ben. God fucking dammit—of all the cruel tricks, all the horribly mean karmic games to play on me, that's the one I can't stop thinking about.

From the moment I woke up in this strange place—and honestly, I don't know where that is exactly, as I've not seen the sun for days. And for days, I am cloistered, tucked away in Carol and Gary's den of iniquity, come to life in North Georgia like a painting of Hieronymus Bosch, only to be knocked out and imprisoned until they summon me for my naughty talents once again.

I'd pray for guidance and strength if I believed in the same God I prayed to in my childhood. Somehow, me being the tool of Satan's minions now, I have a feeling my prayers will fall on deaf ears.

I miss Meghan.

Whatever she's done, I miss her.

I want to punch her in the face, of course, but I miss her. This reversal of fortune feels like a bad dream. I'm still hopelessly her fool, and I can't help that I'm waiting for someone to wake me.

I feel so small. I am afraid, and that's not who I want to be.

And then there is the full moon.

The wind blows, and my skin ripples with tiny pin-prick tingles as I look up at it. Maybe when I fall asleep, I tell myself, I'll wake up and she'll be there spooning me, kissing my neck, telling me I was having a nightmare.

How did I get here?

I look up at the sky.

Gemini. Virgo. Scorpio. Countless stars.

I want to talk to the black sky with her seminal pearly earring, the Night Goddess. She breathes through me and inside me. I am the womb for her song, the one to remake me into her god.

Remaking.

I sit in the grass, ignoring the wet cold blades tickling my undercarriage, and I close my eyes. I picture myself in the sky with the Night Goddess. I dwell above the earth with her and take her as my lover in a bed made of stars. We fuck in the cosmic sea until dawn for all time. Each night, I dip into the liquid blackness below me to rearrange Orion and Leo and set loose the Big Bear to trample the Milky Way.

Here do I remake the constellations.

Here do I remake the hours of waiting and wondering and wandering.

Here do I remake my love for the Night Goddess, who betrayed me, who drew my soul from the pit of Hades as if I were a woman called Eurydice.

Here do I remake myself into Orpheus instead.

Remaking.

And so it comes to pass that, in the afterglow of lovemaking, after the Night Goddess hands me a bowl and bids me to drink deep of the Moon's water, after she has toyed with my devotion and love, I swallow the liquid in that vessel. I set myself on fire.

Remaking.

She laughs at my lust, my burning loins, and leaves me, dropping below the horizon to dance for other unwary gods on the other side of the world.

As for me, I imagine my loins burning hotter and brighter. The fire consumes my legs and waist, my chest and face. I am a fiery ball of spinning flame, and I forget the night and the goddess who dwells in it, for I am now become a new god, one for a new day.

"What the fuck am I going to do now?"

I whisper the words to the wind.

There is no reply, so I hang my head and weep.

The tears are loath to come as easily as my orgasms, so I throw back my head and laugh.

"I'll remake my shape then," I tell the moon. "Fuck you, night. I'm a grown-ass man sitting naked in the grass in the middle of the night talking to myself like a lunatic."

The snap of a tree branch to my right announces my uninvited visitor. "Sometimes, the one you love despises you and there's nothing to be done about it."

"Simone?"

Indeed, it is my keeper. Simone emerges from the darkness to sit beside me in the grass. "Aren't you cold?" she asks. "You've been out here for an hour. Your skin's got nipple-sized goosebumps all over. It wouldn't be a good idea to get sick right now."

"Because they'll think I'm doing it on purpose?"

Simone sighs. "Something like that," she says. "Look, I never like the new stud recruits, but for some reason I like you. You're not my type at all."

"What type is that? White?"

She laughs. "You racist fucker—you're a male, and males are not my type," Simone says, adding, "Not usually, that is."

"I like you, Simone, and you're not my type either."

She smiles. "What type is that? Black?"

I smile. "You're a woman," I reply, weakly adding, "and I could give a shit what color you are. If you have a pussy, you ain't my type. For the time being, that is."

"That should make tomorrow easier for you then."

"Simone, I'm here against my will because a woman I loved—a woman I thought I knew and trusted—had me drugged and kidnapped. I'm feeling myself slip into orphan survival mode. Fuck, if I can do it as a kid, I can as a man. Wait, why should a justified distrust of women make tomorrow easier for me?"

"Joss, please," Simone says, her voice filled with worry. "Whatever you went through as an orphan, whatever you did to survive, it won't save you here. You don't know what this place really is outside of what it is for the couples who come here for help. If they knew the dirty secret about BLUE, they'd have this place shut down in a blink. Carol and Gary have deluded themselves into believing the young people they recruit for their sexual healing porn for couples are helped best by working for BLUE. Because no one else can possibly understand her vagabond actresses and actors like Doctor Carol 'Cuntlicker' Rider. There is the legitimate stuff, the retreat facility and lodge—the couples treatment and remaking love programs—and then there's BLUE, where the means justify the ends."

Remaking me into what?

"So, why are you here?" I ask. "Are you an actress?"

Simone looks at me thoughtfully. There's something in her eyes I almost recognize. I wonder if she's hoping I might see it too, but she sighs and turns away her face.

"Don't resist, Joss Parker. Accept your fate and play along. You're an actor, and I hear you're good, so you can pretend to be a porn star until you stop can pretending. Take the fucking pills they give you and do what Gary and Carol tell you to do."

"What if I don't?"

"The stables, and believe me, it's a place you don't want to be."

"You keep repeating yourself a lot, Simone."

"Because you're not listening to me! You can't escape, you're stuck here—so, enjoy the drugs, enjoy the sex, enjoy the spotlight attention, enjoy being young and famous, enjoy the freedom it will buy you. When you hit thirty and you're too old for this, you can rebuild your life. Do what they say. Give them what they want from you. After your face and body and name are done, they'll let you walk away a very rich man."

"Is that what Meghan's doing?"

"For almost a year now," Simone replies, seemingly disgusted. "She's quite popular—her movies sell more copies and generate more web hits than all the other actors and actresses combined. Apparently, Carol and Gary think you'll do better."

"She's lost to me, isn't she?"

"She's never wanted anyone to find her," Simone says, sadly as she turns away. "When Carol and Gary were finished with her therapy, they told me she was the key to finding the next crop of star performers. Apparently, she's a magnet for people like herself who aren't capable of having a loving relationship because they aren't capable of being happy. Period. She recruited you and another young man to the ranch at their request."

"Another one? Who?"

"I haven't processed him, but I hear he won't be ready to be filmed until tonight—he won't know he's being filmed, which is why they have scouts lure their prospects with love and promises of reunion, and other lies that people of a certain type desire." She holds up my folder and tosses it back to the desk. "I'll see him in a day or so, depending on how his body reacts to the drugs."

What the hell have I done?

Simone stands up. "Listen, I can't stress enough that you need to DO WHAT THEY TELL YOU." She helps me to my feet. I half-expect her to look at my naked body, but she doesn't. Or so I think until she says, "If I weren't mostly lesbian, I'd seriously consider licking you from crack to crack on a sweaty day. No man has ever put those thoughts into my head but Saint Tim Tebow, so consider it high praise. You and Gary will be filming a scene together this week, with the new guy Bilouxi recruited."

"Bilouxi? Who's that?"

Simone walks me to the glass door and ushers me inside my room. "Meghan goes by Bilouxi—she has for a year now. She only used Meghan for you. Get used to name changes, Joss. You'll have a new one too. I left you a sedative that'll get you a solid eight hours. I'll be back to take you to the studio for breakfast with Gary."

"What am I doing with that bastard?"

"Helping him write a script for your shoot later this week," Simone replies. "It's from a story I wrote last year for BLUE Magazine—I'm the editor, so I get to feature my own work when I'm inspired."

My heart starts beating. "What inspires you?"

She smiles. "Does it matter what I enjoy writing?"

"Yes."

"Listen, I spend most of my days tits-deep in a pool of naked men," Simone says. "I need a way to expunge my brain of those images, so I type words into my laptop and send my stories out into the ether. It's cathartic for me."

"Great, Simone," I say.

"It's different from the kind of story you performed the other night, Joss," she tells me, touching my arm in sympathy. "It's more intimate, more honest."

I shake my head. "And very gay."

"You just said women weren't your type," Simone offers, trying to lighten my mood. "It won't be so bad if you focus on the love parts in the story. It'll help you write a good script if you focus your energy there. A good script will make it easier for you to pretend in front of the camera—you won't be on heavy drugs this time, so help Gary write a good script. Oh, blood tests—one a week starting tomorrow. No condoms on BLUE films."

"Thanks, Simone."

"Don't thank me yet—take that pill and get some sleep," she says. "I'll see you in the morning, Joss. Please try to trust what I am telling you."

"Is this the last time I have my name?"

"Goodnight, Joss Parker," she says and closes the door.

No, I don't take her pill.

And no, I don't trust or believe her.

Love, she told me to focus on the love.

Fuck you, love.

Love is dead. Love is obsession and a need for possession. Love is a word we use that allows us to indulge in our lusts. Thinking love is a light in the darkness is madness. In the end, love isn't merely the word for a feeling. It is a drug, the name of the doorway leading into the underworld. My foster mother used to say, "On the ninth day God accidentally created misery because he purposefully created love on the eighth."

I remember her repeating that phrase, but I never understood it until this moment. The anger I normally feel keeps my tears locked deep in the wells of my eyes, but with my body in such a weak state… I crawl into my cot and get under the sheets. I weep myself into a deep sleep.

I didn't need a pill to knock my ass out—I am simply and utterly that exhausted. I wish I could say I don't remember the dreams when Simone collects me in the morning.

I wish I could say I put my trust in her.

I wish I could say I dig down deep and prepare myself to do everything she told me to do.

I wish I could say it.

But anyone who knows me knows that I'm a stubborn fuck on my best day, and that's when no one tells me what I should or shouldn't do. I'm sure you can imagine things aren't going to work out so well for me.

*

Bottoms Up

> *The penchant for sodomy is the result of physical formation we cannot alter. Sometimes it is the fruit of satiety; but even in this case, is it less Nature's doing? Regardless of how it is viewed, it is her work, and, in every instance, what she inspires must be respected.*
>
> —Marquis de Sade, from *Philosophy in the Bedroom*

IT'S AN HOUR AFTER BREAKFAST. I'm sitting in a dimly lit studio—above or below ground, I don't know. I haven't seen the sun in days, and I can't offer too much by way of describing my environment in its entirety.

The room is large, about a hundred feet wide and long, maybe twenty or so feet from floor to ceiling. There are no windows. The only light comes from the four tall lamps in each of the corners.

It's like a black box theater.

There's one table, two chairs, our dirty breakfast plates stacked on the floor next to the only door into or out of the room. There's a two-way mirror and an intercom next to it. But the most curious thing about the place is the winding rail system bolted into the high ceiling. At first glance, it looks like the kind of system dry cleaners use but twice the size. The contraption takes up half the room and works like a ski lift, but instead of chairs there are evenly spaced metal pegs on a sliding track.

I can't take my off the thing.

What the hell is that thing for?

My mind is turning over the possibilities as Gary reads aloud the erotic story Simone had written, the one we're going to turn into a script. I'm so distracted that I don't hear him when he tells me to undress and pose as he reads. "I'm sorry," I tell him. "You and Carol have seen my naked ass plenty. You can watch the footage of me shaking it all you want."

Needlesstosay, I don't take off my clothes.

Gary laughs. "I need to see how aroused you get from the erotic passages," he says, shuffling the pages. "It'll help when we rehearse our love scenes this afternoon."

"Aren't we writing a script first?"

"We'll write the script using what works," he replies. "We're not going all-out, so quit with the attitude, and get your head into the story."

I never thought staying with one man for longer than a month or two would be feasible until I met Onyx. I'm fifty-six. I've been around the block. But this guy, he's the One. Anyway, I remember this one Friday evening, and I'm naked on the couch waiting for Onyx to come home. The door opens and in he walks with a grin as wide as my mother's ass on his face. "Gary, I have a surprise for you," he says, as the prettiest piece of man-boy flesh strolls over the threshold.

Gary's not happy when I tell him I hate the name Onyx. And when I tell him I don't want to rehearse before we have a script. He laughs it off, as if I didn't have a say about anything, and orders me to take off my clothes.

"Jesus, I can read you like a book," I spit as I undress.

Gary laughs. "What the fuck does that even mean?"

"I'm the forbidden fruit, the ungettable get, both of which are what drive you mad and make you weak. Alright, I'm naked and swinging free, and I'm ready to write. So, who is the third actor we need for the other part? One of the men I don't remember meeting the other night when you drugged me?"

Gary sighs. "You took those pills on your own volition," he says. "There's a new recruit coming in later. Bilouxi's bringing him."

"Her name is Meghan," I say defiantly. "My name is Joss."

Gary looks at me for a long moment. "Your name is Onyx, you pissant little fuck—I own you, body and soul," he says sweetly before reading another passage.

He moans as I harden inside him. His sucking is gentle and noiseless. Onyx pulls my length deeper into his face. His hands slink up my sides and pinch my nipples as he works faster, never pausing. I look down and Onyx, his deep brown eyes peering at me, begins to toy with my meat, rubbing it over his cheeks, his forehead, his neck. He returns it to the wet heat of his mouth, where I explode with tremendous force.

Walking behind me, Gary slaps my ass. "BLUE needs your talent more than I do, Onyx. To tell you the truth, I wouldn't know what to do with you if we were an item in the real world. You're kind of intimidating, bubba. I'm just trying to prepare you for your new career with us, a dream career for any gorgeous young man in need of a family, I'll add. You'll see the way of things, eventually. If not today or tomorrow, then you'll see after a week in the stables working as a cockmonger, one of Carol's pony boys. Our resident male prostitutes will help you see things clearly, I think. You performed with three of them the other night, and one of those talented men is ready to leave the stables."

"You can't do this to me, Gary—this is fucking illegal."

"According to your psychological profile and toxicology report, you're very dangerous to yourself and dangerous to others. Until you've been properly treated, Onyx, you'll be here for some time," he tells me. "It's up to you, dear boy, how willing you are to make yourself indispensable to BLUE. Your relationship with Bilouxi was doomed at the start—neither one of you are good for anybody. She realizes that truth, and so will you."

"Gary, please don't do this."

He circles me slowly, like a shark, and presses his face to mine. "Onyx, swallow your pride and do what we tell you, or you'll go to the stables and work as a whore. Always on call, always at the ready to service anyone on campus, day or night, rain or shine, twenty-four/seven/three-sixty-five. I shudder to think of you throwing away this opportunity for a stint doing sexual room service. So, here's you at the top after not having to pay your dues. Shut up, reach out, and grab the fucking ring, Onyx. Your job is to fuck and act in these intricately honest vignettes that are erotic, honest, and utterly real to the troubled couples here at our retreat center. Your job is to help us help people heal. Carol and I believe you can be the most successful performer we've had—and it means more money than you can imagine having, Onyx."

"By kidnapping me," I tell him. "By feeding me drugs and fucking the men and women you keep locked up in a stable."

"No, by performing exclusively for BLUE, you undergo an intensive five-year inpatient program to help you face your demons," Gary replies. "And we wouldn't dream of putting our women in the stables—we house our girls elsewhere on campus."

"Fuck you, Gary," I spit. "If I'm the golden boy you and Carol say I am, then you figure out a way to break me with more than empty threats."

Shaking his head, Gary goes over to the laptop. Tapping keys, he hums as he adds letters and numbers. Here's me standing in the middle of this big dark room, hating Gary and Carol, hating

Meghan—no, her name's Bilouxi now. Looming directly above me is the goddamn metal skeleton that suddenly makes me feel more naked than I already am.

I wonder who's on the other end of that last keypunch.

Gary spins in his chair, smiling as he waits for the door to open.

Simone comes in and looks around. Gary gets up and grabs her by the arm, making her wince as he pulls her over to me. "You're his keeper, young lady, so make your little boy understand what he's to do before I put him on display for awhile."

He walks back to the laptop and starts typing again.

Simone shakes her head. "Please, do what he says."

"He wants me to fuck the world under the guise of helping couples heal—they want me to be the face of their gay porn movies," I tell her, grabbing her hands and pleading. "This isn't what I want, Simone. It's not who I am. Please, Simone, help me."

Simone sighs. "If Gary puts you on display then you're one step closer to the stables," she says. "You'll sleep when you're told, eat when you're told, bathe when you're told, assist with every odd job you can imagine. And you'll be part of a team, sharing your space with five to six other men. Do what Gary wants you to do."

I look back at him. "What will they do to you if I don't?"

Simone shrugs. "Don't worry about me."

"What does it mean to be put on display?"

She looks at the overhead tracks. "You're on display up there," she says. "They'll bind your hands and drape you over a peg, and get you moving around the room like a piece of meat. They usually let everyone know when someone's on display. A crowd will come to watch you go round the room. Everyone who works at BLUE is into bondage and spanking and—well, let's just say you'll be into the same thing they are, whether you like it or not."

"Fine," I say.

Simone puts a pill into my palm. "Pop it in your mouth," she says. "It'll take the edge off and help get you through the day without a ride on the rails. Carol won't like it if you take a ride on the rails. She's made you out to be some sort of sex god."

I swallow the pill. Simone smiles that pretty smile of hers, kisses my cheek, and leaves.

Gary takes a deep breath, gathers the pages of the story, walks over to me, and picks up where he left off. Soon, I am happy as a naked clam, which makes me a lot more open about letting my arousal show, which comes often and quickly.

"That's the makings of a good script," I say. "Want to rehearse?"

Gary smiles, but he doesn't answer.

"What am I doing wrong now?"

He shrugs. "I'm not convinced your streak of being a stubborn fuck is over," he tells me, returning the pages to the table. "You need a lesson."

From behind me, several hands lift up my arms as others keep me pinned. I can't move, and I can't see my attackers, as one of them has blindfolded me. My instinct to cover my nakedness is strong and sudden, an impulse that fills me with shame when I try to crouch as an alternative. Snickers from the assailants now pulling me off the ground by the wrists, bound together with a thick fat leather strap. They drape me over one of the pegs on the track overhead and I hang there like an unpainted puppet.

"Clean him up," Gary says. "Make it pleasant—he's been through enough hell."

"Picked a new name for him yet, Gary?"

That was from a voice below and behind me.

"Seattle, dear boy, I have named him," Gary says. "This is Onyx Bloodstone, who is having a hard time adjusting, as you can see. Alright, ponies—soap him down, scrub every crevice, shave him pussy silk smooth, and dye his hair. Please, remove his blindfold when you color those golden locks to black."

"Gary, please don't do this," I tell him, my heart racing as I feel sponges caked with suds scrubbing my feet and legs. "Please, Gary. I'm begging you."

"GAG HIM!" Gary orders. "And spank his sweet round ass for being a naughty boy today. Joss Parker is no name for a stud on MY ranch," he says, clapping his hands. "I mean, physique like a Greek statue, muscular and chiseled, smooth with a beautiful prick, and hair to match your new name and that brooding personality of yours. Put your faith and trust in me, Onyx. Only I can return your freedom to you."

The scrubbing and buffing ends.

"Stop moving, or you'll cut yourself," Gary warns. "That's better now—we use straight razors on my ranch. Barber strapped to the keenest, sharpest edge. Right boys? Be gentle, boys—we've got a thoroughbred here and don't want him scarred."

I feel tears welling in my eyes. I can't speak and I can't see. I feel another barrage of well-placed spankings on my ass and thighs. Someone's large hand moves over my thigh and up to my stomach, rubbing in slow gentles circles up to my chest and face. And then the shaving ends. I can't see Gary, but I know he's standing in front of me. I hear his breathing, and I feel his lust as he inspects my tingling naked body.

"He's smooth enough—Witch Hazel him, and then go get the oils and hair dye," he says, petting my chest and stomach, his fingers lightly brushing what's left of my pubic hair. "A little pain is good for the soul—just a few minutes. We need to replenish the moisture in your skin—the oils will make your body feel new." He traces my navel with a finger and gently cups my balls. "You are going to be a bright BLUE star, Onyx."

I smell Egyptian musk and some kind of warm spice I can't place. The men attending me massage my body with the oil.

And I feel rejuvenated, despite myself.

With a snap of his fingers, Gary has them remove my blindfold. The dye they put on my hair takes a while to set, an hour or so, and they time it by turning on the track and counting the number of times I complete a circuit.

Over six hundred, by my count, but I had my eyes closed half the time and didn't care about accuracy.

Without warning, the rail with me dangling from it stops.

I am lifted off the peg and lowered to the ground. They remove my binds and continue rubbing me down, as if I were a fucking horse. Whistling them away, Gary looks at me and pats my back and says, "Onyx, welcome to the family." He hugs me warmly.

"Welcome to the family, Onyx-honey."

Carol is standing behind me with a big smile on her face. She takes my elbow to spin me around for a quick peek and takes me into her open arms. She rocks me back and forth, humming with joy as she whispers, "Welcome to our family, Onyx." She takes me to the table. "Here, let's take off your gag. You must be thirsty after all that. It's ice water, honey—you drink that up. Your hair looks much better pitch black—we got way too many blond ponies clopping 'round here. Your look is distinct now, brooding and dangerous."

Pretending to enjoy their attention, I let them pull me, poke me, fondle me—I have no more fight left in me to do otherwise. After several minutes of it being just the three of us, I hear a tap-tap-tapping on the door as it opens. "May I come in now?" asks a familiar voice from the threshold.

Gary and Carol wave the shadowy visitor over to our little spot. I know who is walking toward me. I know she what she is about to do and say, so I just take a deep breath and wait for her to step into the light. "Welcome to our family, Onyx," she says, hugging me, shaking violently as she stands on tiptoe to kiss me. "Your black hair makes you look like a fucking Italian sculpture, you're so hot. Baby, I'm so glad to see you."

Carol beams at us. "Oh, kiddies, y'all are gonna make Mommy cry," she says. "And Bilouxi-honey, my Tammy Faye Baker mascara will mess up my white coat. I'm just here for a few minutes between shifts in the lab."

Gary puts an arm around her. "Let's give 'em privacy."

Carol nods. "Y'all should have a proper goodbye."

"Oh, no-no-no. I'll make this quick."

I feel lightheaded, but I wait until the older couple go before I sit. I don't know what to say. Or how to feel. "Why, Meghan?" I ask. "Why?"

She doesn't answer me.

"Meghan?"

"You know my name, Onyx—I'm done pretending to be someone I'm not," she says, voice hard before it suddenly lifts into plastic and bubbly. "Onyx is a name that suits you better than Joss, a weak pussy name for a weak pussy orphan. Onyx is a man's name."

My head starts spinning. "Why?"

"Baby, you'll be happy if you just go with the flow," she says, smoothing my forehead. "Even I was surprised at how quickly I accepted this place." Taking my hand, she sighs and says, "I nearly went insane after you left and had no way of finding you. In desperation, I sought the comforting embrace of a mutual acquaintance of ours. Dear Ben came through for me in my time of need. Unfortunately, I grew to hate him when he told me you bought all my self-portraits, when he told me how to get in touch with you. I guess you needed his comforting embrace more than I did.

"Anyway, there's no need to rehash the past. You'll learn the truth better without me getting all worked up in telling it to you. I know you're going to do great things here at BLUE. I know I'm doing great things. I've never felt more alive than I do working with Carol and Gary Rider."

"Please," I whisper, grabbing her hand. "I want to go home."

Meghan-Bilouxi touches my cheek. "But you're already home, Onyx, and I'm sure you'll feel it soon." She kisses me. "Gotta go—I need to get packed and take the car back to the rental place."

"Where are you going?"

"Atlanta. I start filming tomorrow in Buckhead—it's a great script too," she says, bubbly and excited again. "Simone really knows how to write relationships and sexual heat, you know? I'm sorry I deceived you and tricked you into taking this trip, but it's what's best for you and me. We have a chance to be really good friends now that I don't have to act like I'm still pining over you."

Gary is beaming. "She's an amazing actress—everything about her in front of the camera is beyond believable. How she gets into her film roles—I swear you'd think she was in love with every one she fucks. You're going to be a big BLUE star, Bilouxi. And now that we have Onyx too—we really have a shot at being number one in the industry."

"For therapeutic and sexual healing, of course," Carol adds, the look in her eyes saying otherwise. "Y'all remember that. Our Billie-girl doesn't perform for any other purpose save making all who bear witness to her honesty understand her purity of heart and mind, her dedication to those she loves."

Gary smiles. "It doesn't hurt that she fucks like a minx either."

Carol laughs. "No, Gary-honey, it sure as hell doesn't," she says, slithering toward me, like Mae West in a snake dress. "Onyx, BLUE'S erotic products help broken people reconnect body, mind, and soul. Your job isn't just convincing our couples that you are exactly the way they see you. Your job, my hot little darlin', is also convincing the people outside of BLUE, the people outside of the ranch, the people besides Gary and me. You understand what I'm tellin' you, my pretty-pretty pony? Whether you mostly prefer women is beside the point. Half of our couples are gay men, so you will be their model in every scenario and situation. What you did on screen the other night made us realize you are super human. I swear, you could turn a straight man upside down in lust for you. Don't worry, we'll throw you and my Billie-girl back together for a series of intense workshop films—and wouldn't that be fun?"

I'm on autopilot now. "Yes, I'd like that," I say blankly.

Carol grabs my chin hard, sinking her nails into my cheeks until they nearly pierce my flesh. "Lemme tell you something, fuck stain. If you don't turn your ship all the way 'round and play your role with oomph and gusto for Mommy Carol, I'll put you in my stables for the rest of your young life. There are plenty of hot studs who'd kill their mamas to be in your shoes, so don't think for one second Gary's the one you gotta fear. LOOK. AT. ME. WHEN. I'M. TALKIN'. TO. YOU. That's better. Never forget that I'll eat your cock and balls for breakfast if you keep pitchin' little bitch fits." When she lets go of my face, she touches the head of my flaccid penis. "Even when it's sleeping, this cock of yours is a sight to behold. I'd hate to do something horrible to something so flawless—Billie-girl, say 'bye to Onyx and go fetch me Simone."

"Yes, Carol," was the reply. "'Bye, Onyx."

I watch the woman I once called Meghan leave.

Gary steps back when Simone enters the room.

Carol binds my wrists behind my back and hands me over to my keeper. "Onyx needs a time out," she hisses, turning on her heel and taking her husband by the arm. "Put his naked ass in the stable, the stall next to that blond pony Bilouxi recruited a few months back. You have one week to break this wild stallion, Simone. Don't hold back when you break him either—I can tell by the look in your black lesbian eyes that you got a soft spot for him. Teach him how to behave, or it's YOUR ass!"

The door opens.

As it closes, she tells Gary, "I hope to Christ this works—I'd hate to put down a prizewinning horse before his time."

When they're gone, and Simone and I are alone in the room, I look at her and ask, “What does she mean about you breaking me?”

“It means I’ll break you as I would break a wild horse,” she says. “I fucking told you to listen, Onyx, goddammit. Come along, wild pony. You stupid, stupid fucking pony.”

Simone doesn’t say another word as she leads me from the room and down the hall. I’m lost in despair and sadness, so I don’t pay attention to where I’m going. Several times, I trip over my own bare feet, which seems to annoy my keeper. She’s jerking me harder the closer we get to our destination.

We finally reach the stables, a small wooden barn set apart from the cluster of offices in the studio complex. We go inside. She takes me to a stall at the end of a long row of them and opens the gate. There’s a cot against the slatted wall, a spigot on the wall opposite the gate, and nothing else.

Simone removes my cuffs, tosses me a blanket and pillow, and puts a leather harness over my head. She fastens the straps under my arms and my legs, lightly slapping my balls and ass. She fits two clamps over my nipples, the pain smarting for a long moment before finally ebbing to a dull, warm ache. She puts a collar around my neck and locks it with a key she wears around her neck.

“You fucking idiot,” she says, shaking her head as she closes the gate with a sad smile. “Tomorrow, I start breaking you.”

“Why?”

“Because this is my job, Onyx,” she says, “and I’m very good at what I do.”

"Simone, I'll do whatever Carol wants. Please, help me."

"Dinner will be brought to you in an hour," she says, ignoring me. "You have free reign to roam the space tonight, but only until bedtime. The showers and toilets are in the back next to the weight room. It may look like a farmer's wet dream in here, but it's clean and cozy. I'd tell you to ask your stable-mates to show you the ropes, but I doubt they'll hear you over all the shouting and yelling that's about to happen."

"Why's that?" I ask, my skin tingling with chills.

Simone looks at her hands. "Because all ponies get hazed their first night in the stables, Onyx. See you in the morning," she says, walking away. "Goodnight, my beautiful studs. My beautiful, domesticated, well-behaving ponies. Don't bruise or mark your new brother, do you understand me?"

From the other stalls, excited answers from the others.

"Yes, Mistress!"

"Of course, Mistress!"

"We wouldn't dream of it, Mistress."

"Goodnight, Mistress."

"I love you, Mistress."

"I'll dream only of you, Mistress!"

"Simone," I call out, my voice and panic rising. "Simone!"

But Simone doesn't answer.

"SIMONE!"

The lights dim as the stable door opens. I hear the others shuffling in their stalls until the silence becomes unbearable. When I call out her name one last time, the barn door slams shut. Then I hear the roll of laughter coming back to me in waves of mocking sound. And then I hear teasing growls and wolf whistles.

I sit on the cot and stare ahead of me. I don't know what to think or feel.

And I don't care about the hazing.

One by one, the latches on the other stalls lift. And then their gates open. And then I hear the soft padded footsteps of barefooted men approaching. I can make out their dark shapes beyond the gate of my stall, which slowly opens on creaking hinges.

One voice says, "Gag him."

Another voice says, "String him up so we can paddle him."

A third voice says, "No, boys—give me a moment with him."

I immediately recognize it.

I'm not surprised when Ben steps uninvited into my stall and sits beside me on the cot. He doesn't say another word. He simply takes my hand into his and lets out a heavy sigh. I haven't heard from or seen Ben in months. Now I know why. I can't look at him, but I want to look at him.

"When did she recruit you, Ben?" I finally manage.

He laughs. "Easter weekend," he says, squeezing my hand. "And my name's Seattle now, so get used to it, my dear stupidly gorgeous Onyx. The name suits you. As does your new hair color."

"So, I've heard," I tell him. "Why Seattle?"

He laughs. "Carol says I look like a pretty Curt Cobain," he replies. "Listen, you and I had a history, but it goes away starting now." He whispers low and deep in my ear. "Tonight, we'll make better history." He nibbles on my lobe, and after sucking it, he says, "Don't worry, Onyx. I know what turns you on. Even if you don't know it just yet. Alright, boys—let's show our new wild stallion what being a cockmonger means."

The other young men shuffle into my stall and lift me up. I don't struggle, protest, or beg them to stop.

Why fight the inevitable?

I suspect my week to come won't be an easy one, but I'm not afraid of where it'll take me now.

As my strong harnessed brothers carry me about the barn, their hands moving over my skin, their fingers poking and probing their tongues licking and tasting, their mouths sucking and sighing, their hips sliding and grinding, their hard pricks pressing and pushing, their lusts rising and rising and rising until—

Hours later, as we lie in a pile on the floor, and the steady sighs and snores of my new friends fill my ears, my mind goes back to last night. Back to the moment Simone told me what to do. "Enjoy the drugs, enjoy the sex, enjoy the spotlight attention, enjoy being young and famous, enjoy the freedom it will buy you."

The man I once called Ben stirs beside me. He presses his body into mine. Wraps his arm over me. Kisses my neck, my chest, my collarbone, my armpit, my nipples, my bellybutton, my hips.

His desire for me is evident. And so, as I was earlier instructed, I position myself on all fours and proffer my ass to him. He gets to his feet and helps me up. He takes my hand and leads me to the back of the barn to the shower room. We stand under the metal head protruding from a far wall.

We kiss, fuck slowly. He lets me come this time.

Onyx, enjoy the drugs, enjoy the sex...enjoy being young...

I will, Simone. I promise.

And with that, I let everything go.

But then it begins to rain—oh, how I hate the rain.

*

The Story Continues in Part Two

BLACK & BLUE

BRONWEN PRYCE

ABOUT THE AUTHOR

Bronwen Pryce (1973 -) was born in Topeka, Kansas. For the past fifteen years she's written erotic fiction for various men's publications, gay and straight, in both short and novellete formats. BLUE is the first volume in her Deep BLUE Three trilogy, an amalgam of various erotic genres into a single story told from the point of view of its three main characters. Bronwen Pryce is married and divides her time between Seattle, WA, and Portland, OR.

http://www.amazon.com/Bronwen-Pryce/e/B00PNU54PI

BLUE

First Printing (eBook), 2014. Second Printing, 2015.

ISBN 978-0692430064

Blue Mountain Books c/o DBP Press
Post Office Box 399 | Tarpon Springs, FL 34688

www.ingramcontent.com/pod-product-compliance
Lightning Source LLC
Chambersburg PA
CBHW030251130626
46549CB00002B/483
* 9 7 8 0 6 9 2 4 3 0 0 6 4 *